The Tribes of Palos Verdes

The Tribes of Palos Verdes

Joy Nicholson

St. Martin's Press

New York

•

Acknowledgments

Thank you to *Surfer* and *Surfing* magazines.

And to F.Z.

•

This is a work of fiction. All of the characters
and events portrayed in this novel are either
products of the author's imagination,
or are used fictitiously.

THE TRIBES OF PALOS VERDES. Copyright © 1997 by Joy Nicholson. All rights
reserved. Printed in the United States of America. No part of this book may be used
or reproduced in any manner whatsoever without written permission except in the case
of brief quotations embodied in critical articles or reviews. For information, address
St. Martin's Press, 175 Fifth Avenue, New York, N.Y. 10010.

Library of Congress Cataloging-in-Publication Data
Nicholson, Joy.
    The tribes of Palos Verdes / Joy Nicholson. —1st U.S. ed.
      p.   cm.
    ISBN 0-312-15677-4
    I. Title.
    PS3564.I2774T7   1997
    813' .54——dc21   97-12429
                                    CIP

First Edition: October 1997

10 9 8 7 6 5 4 3 2 1

for Jay

·

Waves

～～～

·

I'm almost fourteen, already in trouble at school, already been kissed. My breasts have formed into tiny peaks, and there they will stay, tiny, for the rest of my life.

My mother tells me people with tiny breasts are always selfish. She says this as she spreads peanut butter on angel food cake slices for lunch. I am looking out the window, counting the waves as they roll softly by, counting the minutes until I may be excused. But my mother goes on talking, looking at a point just over my two breasts and smiling. She talks about thinness, skimpiness, vanishing to the point of nothing.

"I used to be thin. But I overcame it," she insists. "It was all shit."

I am watching my mother eat. Crumbs are dripping from her mouth, a globule of peanut butter is stuck in her hair. Watching her chew, I am overcome.

☙☙☙

Jim is my twin brother, with my green eyes. Except they are murkier, the color of the water in the tide pools below our house in Palos Verdes. Jim is beautiful. He has been my best friend for years, my only true friend. Together we watch the surfers rise from their bellies on a wave, gripping the rails of their surfboards, standing without falling. For years we've known what the other is thinking. We think about water.

~~~~~~

At 4:30 there's a good cartoon on television. A blond girl and a boy are on the beach. The boy is far out in the turquoise water, bobbing happily, doing tricks for the girl who is trying to take his picture with a big cartoon camera. The girl keeps yelling, "Smile!" and the boy keeps smiling at her.

Then a wave comes. A huge wave rising on the horizon, a mountain of stealthy, black cartoon water, far over the boy's head.

When the girl yells, "Wave! Wave!" the boy waves to her. That's when the water crashes down over his head, flattening him thin, like a sheet of paper.

"Wave," my brother repeats, as we laugh at the cartoon.

"What are you two laughing at?" my mother calls from her bedroom down the hall.

I don't answer because I'm afraid she'll come in and sit down between us, talking through the good parts, whispering with my brother. I like it best when it's just me and Jim, and I can braid his baby-soft hair into tiny plaits like a Rastaman. He never lets me touch his hair in front of my mother.

"Don't treat him like a girl," she always tells me. "He's too old for that now."

But Jim calls out, tells her to come in and watch cartoons with us. When she sits down between us, all the air rushes out of the sofa cushion. We all sink low into the flecked canvas.

"You'll like this," he says, grinning at my mother. "Bugs Bunny is on next."

My mother doesn't watch the TV; instead she looks at Jim, smiling.

၅၅၅

"Jim looks more like me all the time," my father says, patting him on the back, drawing up his chest for comparison, "and Medina looks like your mother, exactly."

"She doesn't look a thing like my mother, Phil," my mother says to him. "I don't know why you always say that."

"She looks *exactly* like your mother. Here, look at this photograph."

He drags out a photograph of my grandmother in New York. I look at her beady, black eyes, her tight smile, and her thin arms. I look at her chicken-skin neck. I smile at my mother, move closer to her. She turns to my father, who's sitting next to me in the afternoon shadows.

"Medina looks exactly like you," she says, pulling away.

၅၅၅

On Thursday, the fog blows in while I eat breakfast. My mother is in her bedroom crying, my father is at the hospital. I'm in the kitchen reading the back of a cereal box, waiting for my brother. Then I see him from the window, through the settling fog. He's standing on the driveway, looking around nervously, spraying the asphalt with a hose. When I sneak up on him, he jumps, then yells at me to go back inside. He pushes me, losing control of the hose so it sprays the front of my sweater with cold water. Angry and soaked, I shove him back. He loses his balance, and I hear a big crunch when he hits the ground.

Then I see the graffiti Jim has been trying to erase. A few

girlish chalk marks are still visible on the driveway, left from a graffiti raid on our house the night before.

Medina Mason Sucks.

❧❧❧

Later, my brother floats in the pool, flicking water from his blond hair. In the afternoon haze he is beautiful, shoulders filled out with muscles, not skinny. He says, "Don't you care what the other girls say about you?"

I answer his question with a question. I say, "Do you care what the other girls say about me?"

He thinks for a moment, his tanned arms swishing the water around and around, his head downturned.

He says, "Yes."

I laugh, imagining myself taking off on an approaching wave.

"That's the difference between you and me, Jim. I don't care."

❧❧❧

A chaos of stars is spattered across the skies of Palos Verdes. Everything else is regulated.

Each house must be at least a half acre away from the next, and the grass must be green and cut attractively. All roofs must be made of red tile, and the walls of each house must be whitewashed every three years.

There are laws against loud stereos and rap music. There are laws against pit bulls and loud parrots.

Children must wear uniforms to school, except on "free-dress days," each fourth Friday. The uniforms must be purchased at Palos Verdes Dry Goods, and they are to be kept clean and wrinkle-free.

There are no streetlights in Palos Verdes. There are no sidewalks. The street signs are handmade wood, free of all graffiti, carved in a sweet country scroll.

The air smells of sea oats and eucalyptus leaves. You notice the seagulls, crows, and the low moan of foghorns. If the wind blows from Malaga Canyon you hear the sound of peacocks mating. The eerie wails sound like children crying—

Meeee. Meeee. Meeee.

If you come, you see the lack of streetlights, fast-food stands, and apartment buildings, all outlawed by city ordinance. As you walk through the well-tended parks that are empty except for a few joggers, you see the air is clean.

The Palos Verdes police know each family by name and by make and model of their car. So do the citizens.

∽∽∽

My father loves to drive fast.

Just after we move to Palos Verdes, he buys a Mercedes convertible and takes us on a family drive to see our new neighborhood.

He smiles, careening around the twisty roads, while my mother looks at the huge homes, the tiny ladies. She makes a verbal list of things a woman has to do in order to fit in here: *One,* buy a green tennis skirt. *Two,* lose twenty pounds. *Three,* burn herself to a crisp.

"My God, Phil! Does the sun ever stop!" she exclaims.

My father smooths his flying hair, sweeping his arms

outward in a gesture of pride. "Paradise, no? Didn't I always tell you we'd end up somewhere like this?"

"So thin. Everybody's so thin here, so burned."

"Sandy, the sun is good for you. So is exercise and fresh, clean air."

My mother sinks low in the seat, shielding her face from the light and the thin, thin passersby.

"I can't believe we're living in a place where women wear *green tennis skirts.*"

"You look great in green, Sandy. You'll fit in here in no time at all."

She shrugs, shivering, burying her face in her gray cowl-neck sweater. My father pulls over to the side of the road to put up the top of the convertible.

It is something my father can never get used to, adjusting his life to my mother's sudden darkness.

⌒⌒⌒

It's my first month in Palos Verdes. The moon is full and gigantic; cloud strands float by in the night sky like silvery ribbons. I keep erasing my French homework until the paper is such a mess I can't see anything but smudges. Frustrated, I look out my bedroom window hoping to see sea lions and sea cows. My father says Palos Verdes used to be full of sea lions, but they don't like cars and noise so they've gone away. But sometimes they come secretly in the night, he says, so if I look hard I might see some.

Suddenly I hear a quiet splash. I crawl out on the window ledge, teetering as the wind puffs my pajama bottoms into big pontoons.

That's when I see them.

Eight or ten surfers cut smoothly through the black water, shiny in their rubber wet suits. They move quickly, silently, flashing their cigarette lighters in code as they take their places in the lineup. The first surfer stands up and pushes off. The wave arcs high and topples; I see a shadow race down its face, faster and faster, until it disappears from sight into the black water. I suck in my breath as the wave crashes and an explosion of silver light is thrown up against the moon. Other surfers follow, one after the next, shimmering with speed, melting into the liquid. I hear them laughing in the dark, then taking off again.

The air is wet as I hold my arms out against the salty breeze, imagining, cold air hitting my teeth.

As their lighters get doused, the surfers begin to scream to each other across the waves. Their voices carry clearly to my window.

"I'm fuckin' next."

"You're such a friggin' wave whore."

"Whoooooooooo!"

All order breaks down in the dark. They start to take off two and three to a wave, yelling, badgering each other. They race, paddling fast, laughing and cursing. There's a sharp crack as two boards collide, then silence.

A woman is standing on the edge of the stairs, searching with a powerful flashlight, shining it on each of the surfers, aiming for their eyes, telling them to keep their voices down or she'll call the police.

Immediately I hide from my mother.

My father is a heart surgeon to the stars in Beverly Hills. He removes fatty deposits from famous comedians and handsome-but-aging television stars.

As long as I can remember, he wanted to live in Southern California—the Golden State. The day he told us we'd be leaving Michigan he picked me up, swinging me around and around, almost knocking over the coffee table. He said soon we'd have orange trees, a big pool, and a pretty view of the ocean. There would be clean beaches, dolphins, and whales, and best of all it would never, ever get cold. My mother wasn't convinced. She said California was full of divorced people, murderers, and earthquakes.

∽∽∽

On the plane, coming to California for the first time, my mother sits with my brother, looking out the window. My father talks to me across the aisle, glancing at the red-haired stewardess. He's rubbing his hands together over and over as if washing them.

"Guess what Palos Verdes means in Spanish," he says. "It means *green sticks*. Don't you think that's a funny name for a place, princess?" He looks at the pretty stewardess again, catching her eye and smiling.

My mother looks out the window toward Michigan, ignoring my father's cheerful banter. After a few minutes, she flags down the stewardess.

"My husband would like to meet you," she says.

∽∽∽

In Palos Verdes, if you are close enough to the shore that the waves keep you awake at night, you are admitted to the tennis club, where you can play a set with the Mad Servers and complain about the water.

"It's just so loud. So incessant. I can't sleep."

My mother has plenty to say to the ladies of the Mad Servers.

"The surfers. They destroy all the ice plant. They drag their boards across the ice plant and ruin everything."

The Mad Servers look at each other. A few nod their heads politely. Until she continues.

"What's wrong with this place? How come the children roam around in packs? Why do they gather like mantises on the cliffs?"

This is my mother's first faux pas. The ladies of P.V. don't want to hear complaints about their children. The drinking, the smoking, the violence. No one wants to think about *that*. A kiss on both cheeks, a bibb lettuce luncheon: that is friendship.

∽∽∽

Jim and I have lessons after school. All children are supposed to have lessons in Palos Verdes. There are tennis lessons, drama, and French. Voice, flute, and piano instruction. Lessons for ballroom dancing called cotillion, which surfers attend once a month in full formal dress. They learn how to cha-cha and waltz, so stoned they can barely lead their partners around the floor. Primly dressed girls apply red lipstick in the auditorium bathroom and hike up their long gowns until you see the curve of tanned calf.

There are Hebrew schools for the Jews, catechism for the

Catholics. There are Girl Scouts and horse-riding lessons. Even polo.

Jim and I protest. We say we don't want so many lessons, because there's no time for fun things. I hear my parents talking it over in the kitchen.

"Maybe we should let them play with the other kids, maybe children shouldn't have so many things to do," my father says.

"Who could they play with, Phil? All the other kids have lessons, too."

∾∾∾

The Palos Verdes mothers drive their children to these lessons between their facials and analysis. Or if they have housekeepers who drive, the maids do the chauffeuring. In return, the housekeepers get two hundred dollars a week and first pick of the Goodwill piles.

"We're so happy to help your family in Mexico," the ladies say. *"Take anything in that pile right over there, anything you want."*

∾∾∾

"I know you want it," my neighbor Danny says.

He is fifteen and superweird. He says he'll give me a surprise if I lift up my shirt, let him see. We're sitting in his tree house above the eucalyptus grove in his backyard. Pot is puffing out the sides of his mouth, choking him like an amateur. He stares at my flat chest, choking.

His eyes are red and filmy, his hands tightly clenched over the nose of the vanilla surfboard he offers. The board is smooth and pale white, with a single flame of orange down the left side. It has two fins. Two. Danny strokes the board cockily and tells me I have to hold up my shirt for ten seconds if I want it—he'll count.

I think about the ocean outside my window, how I see the guys glide on it. I imagine myself free.

"That's all," I tell Danny. "One—one thousand, two—one thousand, like that. And you have to stay over there."

He eyes the board, then my shirt, squeezing his palms together, stoned, fanning his ugly face in the warm air. He nods, he gestures for me to lift it up.

"First put that board over here," I say.

I watch him put the board in the crook of his arm, carrying it to the place I decree. A place just beneath my feet.

"Now go back there, to where you were."

The whole ten seconds, I look at his eyes, at his dull expression. He stares at my bare, flat chest, saying nothing, blowing air on the inside of his cheeks like a stupid puffer fish.

When it's done, he doesn't look at me. He lies down on the wooden floor, breathing hard, dizzy. He motions for me to come to him, but I run, putting the vanilla board in the crook of my arm, dragging it down the rope ladder, smelling its coating of coconut wax and resin. All night I think about it, sitting in the garage, waiting for me to hold it.

After breakfast the next day, I avoid my mother and her dark sunglasses and heavy silences, but I sneak my brother out to the garage and show him the vanilla board. I run my fingers over its nose, talking about water. I promise I can get him one. I cross my heart.

Then I go to Danny in his tree house, climb right up the ladder as if it's mine.

"I want another," I insist. "I want another board."

He doesn't look at me, but he says he will talk to his friend.

The next day I go to Adam Frankel's house. Adam Frankel is sweaty, nervous, clammy. He tells me three times that his mother is coming home soon. His giant Adam's apple strikes me as funny, so I laugh and laugh. Then lift up my shirt, still laughing.

My brother's new board is green like his eyes.

❧❧❧

The next day is free-dress day. The popular girls are all comparing their pretty outfits, doing a mock fashion show under the awning. I smile secretly, thinking of my surfboard as I sneak past them in the concrete hallway. But the girls come to hover around me, laughing, trying to trip me with their feet. I walk past, float even, as Cami Miller shouts out, "Five dollars!" eyeing my favorite brown pants.

Adelle Braverman follows suit, yelling, "Six ninety-nine!" and spitting at my pretty leatherette thongs.

I flinch only when Cami almost hits me with a heavy science book. As I jump back, Cami says, "Don't worry, we aren't gonna hit you. We wouldn't touch such a dirty girl."

❧❧❧

I feel clean later, lying in the pool on my board for the first time. Cami is on the beach, a million miles away. I curse her as I float through the deep end, scanning the stairs for Jim, so he can hold my ankles if I try to stand up.

As I wait, I paddle slowly, back and forth in a line, maneuvering through the flat water on my belly, humming to myself.

I'm going to be the only girl to surf Palos Verdes.

Sometimes I dream I'm a boy.

∽∽∽

The next day I carry my board, balancing it on my head down the cliff stairs to the bay. Jim follows, embarrassed, dragging his board under his arm like a suitcase. The water is calm and flat like the circle in a turquoise ring, but Jim bites his lip, scanning the horizon.

"People will laugh, maybe we should learn somewhere else."

"Oh Jim, don't be such a pussy, just close your eyes and go in."

For a minute I think he is going to punch me, but instead he smiles.

"You're insane, you crazy girl."

He slaps me hard with a frond of seaweed. Together we fight, kicking water into each other's nostrils, struggling to push each other into the whitewash. I jump in and climb on the board, holding its rail down with one hand the way pro surfers do. Jim jumps in, too, and pushes me off. I flounder in the water angrily, spinning and defeated.

"You surf like a girl," he says.

"You suck," I say, "like a troll."

He puts his right foot forward, and then his left, and says, "Which way are you supposed to stand?"

As I think about this, I forget how mad I am.

"Whichever way feels better," I tell him.

CRACRACRA

"Do you have the face you deserve after thirty?"

My mother cuts this quote out of a magazine and pastes it to the refrigerator. My mother is thirty-four. My father is forty-one.

My father looks at the quote and laughs, gathering my mother in his arms.

"You don't have to worry about that," he says. "When the times comes, I know doctors who can make you look twenty again."

"Maybe they can just replace my head," she says, pushing my father away. "Or maybe they'll just replace me when no one's looking."

CRACRACRA

My mother was a model at Bluff's Department Store in Michigan when she met my father. She had what her agency called "the look of the moment."

Like Jackie Kennedy, my mother kept her eyes shrouded in huge, black, oval sunglasses all day. She hated the agency's endless nagging about her waistline, the exercise classes they sent her to, and the diet pills they gave her. But it's easy to see she loved the attention.

Here's a picture of my mother when she was skinny. Jim keeps it in his room, in a white frame on his desk. My mother's sitting on a knoll in a park, her legs demurely crossed, hands on her cheeks. She wears a white French suit, rosette beaded pumps, and a slender gold watch. She is surrounded by cute male models, each holding out a long-stemmed rose for her. She smiles giddily; there are so many flowers, she cannot choose among them.

It is an advertisement for the spring suits of 1964.

Today her hair is still styled like Jackie Kennedy's was in 1964.

∽∽∽

My mother eats in secret while my father is at the hospital. First she only eats salty things that come in bags or plastic boxes. The sweet things come later.

After school and my lessons, I come home to the smell of plastic bags, salsa, and American cheese, all melting in the double oven. Torn tendrils of Dorito packs litter the stovetop, stinking like crossed wires as they melt on the coils.

My mother comes from her room only to get more bags, smiling blandly at me and Jim. Through the walls, we hear the sound of bags being popped open.

She puts an unopened bag of chips in her lap and claps her hands over the mouth of the bag so that it explodes open jauntily. Then it is quiet, until enough time has passed, and then there is another clapping sound, and then more quiet.

Puggles the dog stays in my mother's room, eating the crumbs that explode from the top of the bag. Puggles likes chips very much and wags his tail at the sound of any ripping plastic, even if it is only Dr. Phil Mason, our father, unwrapping a fresh batch of dry cleaning.

My mother gains weight quickly. Her Swedish cheekbones completely dissolve as her waistline expands.

"Don't hurt her feelings," Jim says when I stare.

∽∽∽

My mother met my father when she was eighteen. She was a model, and my father was in medical school. Their parents said they were too young to get married, but they eloped to Chicago and called from a pay phone outside the county courthouse. My mother said she didn't want to get married, but my father says it was like this: When he found out she wasn't really pregnant, it was too late, they were married already.

When I ask why they didn't get a divorce right away, my father sighs. Then he tells me love is like the ocean. It goes far deeper than people understand.

∽∽∽

Nobody likes a new girl. When we first came here from Michigan, everyone laughed at my fancy white boots. When the girls tried to trip me, rolling their eyes, I knew it would be the same as it was in Michigan, even though my father said California would be different. The girls would never accept me, and I'd eat lunch alone again.

I knew Jim would be popular though, and the pretty girls would try to steal him. When I ask him to prick his finger, become my blood brother, he tells me I'm getting fruity.

"We already have the same blood, stupid. We're stuck with each other."

∽∽∽

Today there's a new girl at my school from Vermont. She's very pale, with a delicate face and wavy brown hair. She smiles shyly at me as we each eat our lunches alone on the grass. I don't smile back at her, but she introduces herself anyway, telling me her name is Laura. I chew and nod silently, not giving my name. Then I notice her arms are turning pink in the sun.

"Maybe you should move to the shade," I say, finally.

"I wish I wasn't so pale. The girls are all calling me Casper behind my back," she confides.

"Isn't there any sun in Vermont?" I say. When she flushes, I amend myself quickly. "When we moved here I was su-perwhite, too."

As she smiles again, I look her up and down, appraising.

I say, "No offense, but no one wears a blouse. The teach-ers don't care if you wear a white T-shirt under your uni-form."

"Oh," she says, blushing.

"It's no big deal, just F.Y.I."

When the end-of-lunch bell rings, she puts out her hand for me to shake. "We could meet at snack period," she says, hesitating, "or would you rather eat alone?"

When we meet at snack period, I tell her about the Bay-boys. "They're the best surfers at Lunada Bay. I'm gonna surf with them, even though I'm a girl."

She nods her head and starts to tell me all about her horse. But I interrupt. "Riding waves is way better than rid-ing horses."

Then I demonstrate, imitating the Bayboys, standing up on the rickety bench. "See, the water tries to push them side-ways, but they lean back and put their arms out, like this," I say.

When the bell rings, I say, "I'd invite you over after

school, but my mom's sick." Then I invite her to the beach, after my piano lesson.

"Okay," she says, wrinkling up her nose like a baby rabbit.

The rest of the day I make big plans. Maybe we'll have sleepovers at her house, with popcorn and movies. We'll rent *Endless Summer,* the best surf movie of all time. By the time school's over, my stomach is twisted into happy knots. But as we walk through the gate, Cami Miller walks up behind us, leading a small group of girls, flipping her blond hair.

"You don't want to go with her," Cami whispers. "Medina Mason is the weirdest girl in the whole school. No one likes her."

Laura hesitates, looking at me and then at the other girls.

"I don't care what you do," I say softly, closing my eyes, praying.

When I open them again, she's walking off with Cami's group. She's laughing, wrinkling her ugly nose.

In between periods the girls corner me as I do my homework in the bathroom. Big Annie holds me down while Cami hands Laura a bottle of glue.

"Do it," Cami says, eyes shining.

Laura takes the bottle, trembling. She starts to squirt glue into my hair, but her hand shakes so hard she drops it on the cement floor. When Big Annie bends over to pick the bottle up, I kick her in the ass, knocking her flat. I lock eyes with Laura, raising my hand high over her head, fist wavering, tears in my eyes. Then I stab Cami with a No. 2 pencil. I jab it so hard the lead breaks off in her arm.

Instead of giving me detention, the principal sits me down in the anteroom of his office, shuts the dividing door, calls my father at the hospital. I watch through the cracked, yellowing Plexiglas as he talks on the phone; frowning, nodding his head, doodling on his calendar. After he hangs up, he opens the door, tells me to come in. He clears his throat, adjusts his glasses. He says he knows how difficult it is to be a scapegoat.

"But when the girls provoke you," he says, patting my arm, "try humming a song."

༄༅༄

My father sends me to a famous psychiatrist in a big, mirrored tower.

"What is it about you that the other girls don't like?" he says, pad of paper and studious pen in hand. "Did you have a falling out with one of them?"

"*Fuck* them," I answer. "Girls never like me, and I don't like them."

Scribbling away, the bearded man tries again.

"Are you close with your brother?" he asks.

"Fuck you."

He prescribes children's tranquilizers. But he's the crazy one.

༄༅༄

At home, after my piano lesson, my fingers are sore from banging the piano keys too hard. I pick up an empty cellophane package and show it to Jim.

"Mom ate another whole bag of Oreos today," I say. "I found this in the trash."

"Don't act like a poor person, Medina," my brother says, sighing as he turns up the volume. "Only poor people count how much food there is."

"You don't care how she acts. Even if she eats like a pig!"

My brother throws the channel changer hard against the carpet and yells, "If you talk about it, it'll make it worse!"

As I pick up the dislodged batteries, I breathe hard and concentrate on inserting the shiny shapes between the nest of wires. My brother leans over, gently taking the channel changer away, folding the batteries exactly into place.

"Sorry for throwing it at you," he says, then makes a frog face that usually makes me laugh. When I don't even crack a smile, he twists me into a half nelson, tickling me until neither of us can tell if I'm laughing or crying.

I don't say anything to my mother about the Oreos. Instead I throw away all the junk food in the house, but my mother grabs her car keys from the foyer, leaves the house, and returns later with a stuffed brown sack. She smiles at me and toasts me with a can of chocolate Yoo-Hoo.

She says, "Yoo-Hoo, skinny, Yoo-Hoo, I see you."

⌒⌒⌒

In my mother's checkbook ledger, there are hundreds of checks written out to Ralph's Market, sometimes more than one a day. My father looks through the ledger, shaking his head, pounding his fist on the table.

He tells Jim and me to go to our rooms, but instead we hide behind the door, cupping our ears to its wooden skin. My mother yells at my father. She says she wants to leave Palos Verdes before the sound of the waves drives her crazy.

"That's what you said about Chicago wind and Michigan snow, Sandy. Verbatim."

My mother cuts him off, tells him he better find us a nice,

normal place to live before it's too late. She insists it's the waves that are the problem.

"You promised to get the eating thing under control, Sandy. You said you'd stop the visits to the fridge at night." My father puts his palms together reasonably. "I'm concerned about your health!"

"Oh yes, *my health*." My mother smiles. "I'm sure that's the *real issue* here."

"Heart disease is something I know a thing or two about, Sandy."

"You don't care about my health, Phil, you care about my cheekbones."

As he walks out, she calls out to him.

"I know a thing or two about cheekbones."

⌒⌒⌒

I'm lucky it isn't winter yet, that's when the waves get big in Palos Verdes. The waves are small and swashy now, two feet, perfect to practice on. For the first hour, I concentrate on pushing myself upward as the wave is in motion. Only the third time I try, I stand up and ride the wave to the shore, wobbling but not falling. When the wave ends I know I'll always be a surfer. I know I'll be trying to catch that feeling for the rest of my life.

Jim is stronger, he pushes his body easily upward. But my balance is a little better, I stand up faster, and stay up longer once I catch a ride. I practice every day, even when the local guys paddle out but Jim goes back to shore, embarrassed, swimming fast.

My plan is to be good by December. It's hard to imagine

riding big winter waves that tower over my head, but I try to see myself dwarfed by water, zooming across on the diagonal, the lip closing down behind me.

My father gave me a magazine article about a famous woman surfer in Florida, Frieda Zane. She says the only way to get good is to forget you're a girl, and surf like a man, aggressive and fierce. She says to hang around with better surfers as much as possible, study the way they stand and move, and ignore them if they laugh.

"Don't limit yourself to being a lame chick in the water," she says. "Use your mind—and your arms."

I cut out a picture of Frieda surfing a big, green, velvety wave in Hawaii and hang it over my bed, where I look at it every night before I go to sleep.

Freida doesn't explain exactly what to do when other surfers laugh. Sometimes they catcall across the water, imitating me when I push off. *"It's a UFO,"* they yell, *"an unidentified flailing object."*

I pretend I don't hear them, but I do.

༄༅༄

Palos Verdes is on an earthquake fault line unrelated to the famous San Andreas.

"We have our own fault line," people like to say, "just like we have our own police force and school system."

Because of cliff erosion, entire streets on the west end of the peninsula shift about a foot a year, causing sewage problems and huge cracks in the foundations of houses. But Palos Verdes is listed in almost all travel guidebooks as one of the most beautiful coastal regions in America, so the residents stay, despite the certainty their houses will need extensive repairs every four years. The children of these residents learn that money fixes everything, even nature, if there is enough of it.

⌒⌒⌒

There is the smell of fast food in every room of our house, even though a housekeeper cleans daily. The bathroom smells like meat. The hallways close to my mother's room smell like French fries, cheese, steaks. A heavy oil smell hangs like fog over the carpeted corridor, mixing with the odor of chemicals from nitrogen-flushed bags.

Lately my mother doesn't allow the housekeeper into her bedroom to clean. "My husband is always in someone else's bedroom anyway," she says, listening to the peacocks cry.

"Mating, Phil," she says. "I hear you mating."

⌒⌒⌒

I'm on my stomach in the bay, on my surfboard, experimenting with ways to paddle out faster. The waves are getting bigger now. It seems impossible to get out to the wavebreak because the whitewash keeps pushing me back.

"It's harder for a girl," Jim tells me. "Your arms aren't strong enough."

Even though I get mad, I know it's true. When I try calling a surf shop to ask if there's a secret trick to good paddling, the guy who answers laughs. "Pretend there's a great white comin' at you, girlie." Then he laughs again and hangs up.

First I try pushing water through my fingers like I'm doing the breaststroke, but the board keeps going sideways.

Next I try using my hands like scoops, feeling salt stinging the scabby spots near my bitten nails. Finally, I try pushing the water with my hands and kicking my legs, but my knees keep banging on the hard resin.

Soon I'm sweating in the rubber, but I can't take my wet suit off, because there's nowhere to put it. Sweat and salt water start dripping in my eyes, and I punch the water as hard as I can. The rubber is suffocating me so I unzip the top of my wet suit and balance it on my head, wearing only a cotton T-shirt now.

Then I get an idea: I imagine I'm a machine—a paddling machine that never gets tired. I plunge my arms about a foot into the water and propel myself forward, counting out loud, "One, two, one, two." I paddle across the entire bay faster than I've ever done it before. The only thing that stops me is a gulp of sea water I breathe in by mistake.

Choking, exhilarated, I rest for ten minutes, floating on my back. When I look up at the window, I see my mother's yellow bathrobe reflected in the glass. I wave slowly to her from across the water. Then I put the wet suit back on my head and paddle again, showing off my form.

When I look up a few seconds later, she's gone.

∾∾∾

The other girls have small purses or backpacks, but I carry a silver plastic shopping bag, big enough to hold my wet suit, so I can change in the bushes on the way to the cliffs.

The girls laugh, they point, they titter. As we all wait for the bus after school they cup their hands in perfect unison, together in tribes, planning pranks to play.

"Can I sit here?" Cami Miller is gesturing to a place beside me at the bus stop. A place that is always empty. I ignore her grandly, picking at my nails, humming.

"Well, can I sit here?" Cami repeats, looking at the other girls, smiling, winking.

"Sure," I finally say, "do whatever you want."

"But I don't want to sit here," Cami says, giggling, then laughing tiny silvery bells. *"I don't want to catch anything."*

The other girls laugh, in a gaggle. I think of them washing away. I throw my hands out in a wave.

"Die," I tell them. "Whatever."

Cami is five times as pretty as me now, but she wasn't always. She only got beautiful when she went to Dr. Rosen for a nose job. All the towel girls go to Dr. Rosen. They tape their chins and ears, sometimes they even get their eyelids ripped open and reshaped into half moons. Tara Pugh had her lips enlarged with fat from her own butt.

There are horror stories of plastic surgery gone wrong, like Mrs. Ambrose, whose face caved in from too many reductions, or poor Steph Stone who chose a nose too small for her face and ended up looking like a devious elf.

"But that's because Dr. Rosen didn't do the surgery." The towel girls agree, *"You get what you pay for."*

"I mean, he was like a doctor from Afghanistan or something— from, like, a Third World country or something."

තැම

My father says if I want to make friends I have to start wearing nice clothes. He surprises me with pleated skirts, floral dresses, and little pink socks.

"You don't want to wear those old things; you'll look much better in this," he says, handing me a dress with clumpy purple flowers all over the front.

He has clothes for my mother too, a few sizes too small.

"I'm not an eight anymore," she says, "I'm a sixteen."

"You looked good as an eight." He holds a chic, slinky dress against her frame. Then he pats her hand.

"I want you to see these clothes as a symbol of encouragement. You can lose weight again, Sandy. I know it."

"Why don't you give it to one of your *secret friends,* Phil," she hisses, flinging it aside.

"Mom looks fine," Jim says.

"Thank you, lamb." She lifts an eyebrow at my father.

❧❧❧

"Why don't you wear your new dress to your French lesson?" my father asks me later.

"Yeah, why don't you?" Jim says, trying not to laugh.

"You'll look like a princess in it," my father says, grinning.

"She's not filled out enough for that dress," my mother cuts in. "It'll make her look like a scarecrow."

"I'll wear it," I say quickly. "I like it, Dad."

My mother says, "She's a good liar, like someone else I know." She looks directly at my father.

"I'll *wear* it," I say, again.

I wear the dress out of the house, but I sneak into the garage to change into shorts. Even though I feel guilty, I hide the dress inside the teeth of the lawnmower, next to the Goodwill pile.

I look best in my new wet suit, anyway. Jim tells me I look like a pro.

If I couldn't surf, I'd just die.

Surf or Die. I have a sticker on my notebook that says this.

~~~~~~

Today Jim gets the first wave. We're at the bay, the surf is three feet, no one is out but us. He stands, leaning too far forward, then straightens out. I count six seconds, then the soft flannel sea parts for him. I watch him fall and emerge wet, gasping for air. The salt spray drips heavily, the air is clean and fresh.

I swim for his hat, which bobs a few feet away, his favorite black hat that says P.V. Sea Kings. I present it to him, slapping him on the back, telling him he'll be the greatest surfer that ever lived. I tell him how much I love him.

I tell him he is God.

"We're gonna rule the world," I say. "You'll be the king."

"And you'll be the queen," he says.

"No," I say. "In our world there'll be two kings."

~~~~~~

Surfers live by the rules of the wind and moon, because the wind controls how big the waves are, while the moon pulls the tide back and forth like a puppet on a string.

I'm explaining tides and currents to my mother as I wash out my wet suit in the kitchen sink. She wears her bright yellow bathrobe and dark oval glasses, even though we're indoors.

"So now you respond to the moon?" she says.

After school she sits my brother and me down. She lists

all the things to beware of in the ocean: sharks, rays, rip-tides, jellyfish, and especially unpredictable currents.

As she speaks, she gets very sad, her breathing ragged and rough.

"I'm losing your father," she says, looking at Jim. "I don't want to lose you, too."

Then she shuts the curtain, blacking out the ocean. "Stay where I can see you," she warns. "Don't go too far."

∽∽∽

"Fuckin' ole," Skeezer Laughlin, the biggest and meanest of the Bayboys, says to Jim at the cliffs. "There's gotta be a storm from Mexico pretty soon."

The Bayboys are the popular surfer clique in Palos Verdes. They're the only ones who can surf Lunada Bay, the bay in front of our house, without getting hassled. Jim's always nervous when he sees the Bayboys paddle out; he doesn't know if it's okay for us to surf with them, even though we're locals. As soon as they paddle out, he comes in, trying to make me follow.

Jim nods to Skeezer, acting nonchalant. His fingers pick at the skin around his nails.

"Have a toke?" Skeezer offers Jim a joint, ignoring me. Jim drags hard, and looks out at the water. I see the veins pop out on his neck, but his expression is neutral. Both of them sit there, saying nothing. Skeezer passes the joint to Jim again. I hear a sucking sound, then a high squeal as a massive intake of smoke causes Jim to choke. Skeezer laughs, and starts to choke, too.

"See you at the bay one of these mornings," Skeezer says,

walking away. "And by the way, it would be cool if you let us use your cliff stairs."

On the way home Jim is flushed, quiet. The bitten skin around his nails is bleeding. He wipes his fingers on his shorts.

"We can surf with the Bayboys now," I say. "If Skeezer says we can."

"I heard," he says sharply.

"So do you think we should go out with them tomorrow?" I ask, very excited, poking him in the ribs.

"Maybe we're not good enough to surf with them yet," he answers nervously.

But he's flexing in the mirror when I spy on him later.

౿ఄ౿ఄ౿ఄ

This is how to be a wavegetter in the morning lineup. Set the alarm for 5:30 A.M. in order to do a wave check by six. If you're late, you'll have to take the last spots with the other sleepyheads, and you probably won't get a turn.

If you try to sneak a ride, the Bayboys will get mad and careen their boards at you like big, dull arrows.

Our first morning out with the Bayboys, the waves are flat and unrideable. Jim and I paddle toward the lineup, sweating in our rubber jackets. Skeezer gives my brother the secret handshake and nods to me. He tells me to get in line behind all the guys.

"Ladies don't go first here," he says.

I clear my throat. "I guess you don't get special privileges then."

No one laughs. Nervous, I look at Jim. He keeps his eyes

on the horizon, frowning just the tiniest bit. Finally one of the older guys cracks up and motions for me to line up next to him.

"She got you, Skeez," the guy says.

As I paddle past, Skeezer grumbles, "Hell, from the waist up she could pass for a guy anyway—a real ugly one, though."

Because there's no waves, the guys spend the morning telling their best surf stories—like the time when Skeezer's cousin's friend saw a great white shark at Angel Point, or the day Jim Dayton surfed with Jimmie Ho, the legendary Hawaiian. No one talks to me much. Still, I feel pretty great.

When the waves start to pick up after the school bell rings, Jim and I swim to the shore, hesitating on the shallow sand. Then I decide what to do. I close my eyes and turn quickly back into the water, forgetting about school, even though I'll have to spend a week in Mr. Gross's tardy detention.

I get one junk wave, closing my eyes when I fall. I stay underwater as long as I can so I don't have to hear Skeezer laugh.

ᢙᢙᢙ

Mr. Gross, dean of detention, claims he's dangerous when mad. "I'm a Scorpio, don't cross me," he warns the class today.

He orders each of us to write an honest letter of apology, and turn it in at the end of class for him to read. I struggle over what to write, then decide.

"I'm not sorry at all. I hate school, I hate everything except surfing, and that's the honest truth."

Mr. Gross keeps me after detention the next day. He's very

nice, not like a scorpion at all. He says he has a deal for me; he won't give me extra detention if I rewrite my letter of apology properly.

I write him a letter that says:

> *Dear Mr. Gross,*
> *I guess you want me to lie—*
> *I am sorry for being late.*
> *Medina Mason*

"Thank you, Medina." He takes out a bottle of Liquid Paper, smiling to himself. Quickly he applies a thick white stripe through the middle of my letter so that it says:

> *Dear Mr. Gross,*
> *I am sorry for being late.*
> *Medina Mason*

"I *do* appreciate your honesty," he says, eyes twinkling.

❧❧❧

My brother loves stars. For our birthday, we go to Joshua Tree National Monument where you can see every good constellation in the world. But then my father smiles at a blond lady in front of the Tourist Information Center, and my parents start fighting.

"Why don't you just go to a motel with her right now," my mother says.

"Maybe I will. Maybe I'll just fucking leave."

My brother and I have never heard my father curse out loud before. I laugh, but Jim shakes his head, mad.

"Let's run for it," I say. "Quick! Before Dad drives away!"

I pull Jim with me, running free under a perfect, blue desert sky. "We'll hide from them, make them really sorry," I tell him.

We crouch behind Treasure Rock, giggling as they call our names. I plead with Jim to hide with me all day, telling him we can climb to the very top to scare them, we'll hold hands and pretend to jump.

But when my mother starts to cry, Jim goes to her, head down. He takes her hand, and says he's very, very sorry. When he finally looks back at me, his face is tense like a rubber band being pulled extra tight.

Later that night, Jim shows me the crab formations in the stars. I try to see them, but only see little points of random light.

"Those aren't crabs, really," I say.

He turns, lying on his back on top of a wooden picnic bench, and looks into the sky.

"Those stars there are its head," he says. "See where its body curls around?"

I lie next to him until I think I see a crab with only one pincer.

"What are you two whispering about?" my mother calls out angrily. "Come here, Jim."

Twenty minutes later she's laughing happily, lying in the mouth of the tent with my brother, searching in the sky for The Hunter.

෩෩෩

My father returns at 9:30 in a rental car so he can drive home early. My mother says I have to go with him, even though Jim says it isn't fair. On the way home, my father barely talks. He frowns at me and says, "No, Medina, I don't want to listen to the Rock and Roll Hit Parade."

When he drives very fast, he smiles a little.

∽∽∽

Two days later my brother comes home from Joshua Tree. He's tanned, rested, glowing. He says our mother was in a great mood the rest of the trip; they lay under the stars telling ghost stories, staying up all night.

She even drank a beer, sang Beatles' songs around the big campfire while Jim played guitar. "Can you imagine our mother drinking a beer?" he asks, laughing.

I shrug, jealous, as he describes the fun they had, the moonlight cookouts and visit to famous Loco Rock. At Loco Rock they had a long talk. "She feels so alone here," he says sadly. "The stupid tennis ladies don't like her, and Dad always picks on her." His eyes darken, he balls up his fist, hits the bed in emphasis. "Dad is such a jerk."

"Oh," I say quietly, sick to my stomach.

"She needs a man to protect her," he says fiercely. "When she feels better she'll be normal again."

He warns me to be nice to my mother if I want to keep his respect. He puts his hand on my shoulder, pats it like my father does. Then he smiles shyly, looks at me in wonder. "Mom thinks I'm more of a man than Dad ever was."

∽∽∽

When Jim and I were six, we visited Sky Lake, Michigan, with our father for the day. He was lolling on the sand, looking at the pretty girls stroll up and down the shore in their pastel bikinis, spritzing their hair with lemon pulp, giggling. Watching them untie the backs of their shiny suits, faces to the sand, soaking in hazy sunlight. Watching them and dreaming.

I was a stick figure with buck teeth, but my brother was already perfect. We were playing with blue plastic pails and silver spoons. Making a sand city, just feet in front of the water, a city complete with houses, shops, a zoo. A wave came up suddenly, crashing into the walls of the city, licking away its foundations. Jim dove out of the way, a tear plopping down his chest, his lower lip trembling.

I locked hands with him, dragging him into the ankle-high water, pushing him deeper and deeper. Telling him, "It's just a lake. It won't hurt; don't be afraid."

He followed, toes, knees, thighs, gingerly. The whole time I gave him words of encouragement, holding his hand tightly, not letting him run. Whispering.

"Let's go in, let's go all the way past our necks."

I told him he could have my Mr. Microscope if he'd go in to his waist. Mr. Microscope was our favorite toy; we used it to look at each other's spit, each other's hair.

Then my father came loping toward the water, looking from left to right, making sure the bikini girls thought he was just going for a swim. He spanked me quickly, looking around, smiling at the women, hissing in my ear.

That night, grounded in my room, I looked at magnified tears under the Mr. Microscope, yelling to Jim to come and see, but he stayed away, eating ice cream with my mother. He wouldn't give me anything to examine. He wouldn't give me the time of day. Later I smashed Mr. Microscope and threw it into his room.

❧❧❧

"I don't think you should be such a smartass to Skeezer," Jim
says when we're smoking pot in my room. We're funneling
the exhalations out my bedroom window through a rolled-
up surf poster.

"He's the one who picks fights."

"You've got to give him time to get used to you." Jim
looks at me, biting his lip. "He doesn't like girls surfing.
He thinks it's stupid."

"I think he's stupid," I say. "Plus soon I'll be better
than him."

Jim smiles, his eyes red and swollen. He rolls over on his
belly, and takes aim at me with a rubber band. He asks me
again to please act right in front of the Bayboys.

"If Skeezer says something to you, just keep quiet. It's eas-
ier than fighting him."

"How come you never stand up for me?"

He exhales, long and deep. "I stand up for you all the
time, even when I don't want to."

❧❧❧

My father wants us to be classical pianists, fluent French
speakers, tournament soccer players, and ace students. After
all, he was at the top of his class. He's the first to laugh at
his own jokes, the first up in the morning. He's a runner, a
long-distance jogger, up at five, one foot out of the bed,
stretching before he lunges for the door.

"Got to beat the birds."

That's what he likes to tell us, dewy with sweat, cold and

smiling, after his run, before his wheat germ–banana shake.

He likes to say it's not winning or losing that's important, it's how *quickly* you win. How hard you run, how fast. He slaps us on the back and encourages us to be "the toughest, fastest surfers in Palos Verdes." But I tell him surfing isn't like that.

"How do you win then?" my father asks.

"You just stay on top," my brother explains, irritated.

&smwhwhw;

I'm going fast, flying through air, unstoppable. It's 4:30 after school and there's a freak small swell at Angel Point. It's two to three feet and round, not very mushy. The waves are softly capped, pushing against the bottom of my board, rocking me from side to side.

I'm about to wipe out, but I pretend I'm the wing of a plane, soaring through the air, above trees and rocks and grass. I don't fall off even after I've counted to five. Then I hit whitewash, and the board bounces hard under my feet, as if hitting pavement. There's a thud and I jerk to the left without warning, falling headfirst.

The water slaps my face and chest as I fall, stinging until I land in a soft nest of seaweed. Slippery fronds envelop my legs and stomach as I gasp for breath. My hands are wind-milling wildly until I stop going under.

Before I can reach my board, it's spinning high in the air, pushed by a wave back to the edge of the shore, eddying on the sand in the shallow water.

A piece of hair wraps itself tightly around my neck. An-other wave slaps me in the back, tumbling over my head, pushing my face into the water. When I finally come up again, I'm shaking.

Jim is watching me. He gives me the thumbs-up.

Jim never laughs when I fall.

〜〜〜

I read in *Surfer* magazine about all the different kinds of waves.

Mushy waves blend together like oatmeal. It's hard to stand up in them if they're over three feet. Then they throw you side to side, as if you were bouncing in an earthquake.

Choppy waves push your board up underneath you, so you feel like you're in a blender. They mostly happen on windy days.

Freak swells are waves that come up suddenly, with no warning, unpredicted by the newspaper and 1-900-SURF REPORT.

Cattle waves come right on top of each other. They're dangerous, because there's no time to catch your breath before another one hits you.

Runners are waves too fast to stand on, unless you're a real pro with perfect balance and a knack for speed.

Tubes are the best. High, fast, and shaped like a snug cave, with enough room to stand in. Powerful and rare.

In the winter, the waves at Lunada Bay are tubed.

Tubes are what I dream of.

〜〜〜

I want to be stronger than Skeezer, so I've started doing push-ups, even though I can only do the girl kind, where you keep your legs and pelvis on the floor and lift your upper body with your arms. I've also started jogging, like Frieda Zane, three times a week.

Jim says jogging is stupid, but I like it. Especially knocking low leaves off the eucalyptus trees with my hands and racing the cars uphill. I always avoid the popular kids who gather at the bay at sunset. Instead I veer straight up Rocky Point Road, past the oldest homes in Palos Verdes.

I wave to the fathers as I race their long, silver cars up the road, keeping my hand up for almost half a block, waving at Mr. McCollum, Mr. Wheatly, then Mr. Rider. They work together in the defense industry. Mr. McCollum, a physicist for Lockheed, worked on the B80 bomber. His daughter is the first girl I ever knew who had an abortion.

When the fathers honk in the driveway, their kids try to look less stoned.

"Hi, Dad," they say, stuffing dime bags of pot in their socks, *"what's up?"*

～～～

My mother's yellow bathrobe makes my father very nervous. He says it isn't healthy to wear pajamas all day.

"It isn't healthy to go to the market half naked either," my mother answers. "But I know how you like tennis *skirts.*"

I listen, pretending to do my algebra homework. My father looks up from his medical journals, frowning, unsure of how to respond.

"I see how you look at the ladies, Phil. Always measuring, always trolling for a great pair of . . . legs. That's it, Phil, you're a leg man, not a . . ."

My father picks up his journals and coffee and moves to the guest room. He is good at smooth exits.

～♪～♪～♪

My father says no one is as witty as my mother. He says they used to laugh all the time in the first years of their marriage. Today she's clowning around, reading aloud to me from a copy of the Super Beauty Regimen from *Women Now* magazine.

She mimics the magazine's instructions: "Rub emollient into your skin when it's wet from the shower. Don't forget the problem areas!"

And, "Every woman should examine her body with a cosmetic mirror so she can see her problem areas clearly! Use two mirrors for the backside!"

My mother continues, musing over the Getting Older Gracefully tips: "Cream lipsticks are moister, cotton puffs are gentler, a raw avocado rubbed with circular strokes over the face and chin is the perfect dry-skin mask. *Don't* pull at the eyes and mouth. *Don't* crease the forehead. *Do* glow warmly."

"*Do* go to hell," my mother says, making a face at the cover model.

Now she's looking at a pull-out poster from *In Shape* magazine. The picture is of a beautiful red-haired woman with puffed-out lips and nice white teeth, sitting on an exercise bicycle and smiling. She is my father's favorite celebrity, a very famous model named Rain. He has an autographed picture of her in his office, and a swimsuit calendar, too.

"Do you think this Rain person is prettier than me?" my mother asks, holding the poster close to her eyes.

"No," I say, looking at my shoe.

"Well, your father thinks she's just the bee's knees, Medina."

She says Rain is young enough to be his daughter and asks
if I agree. I look at the picture, trying to decide how old Rain
is. My mother gets angry when I don't figure it out fast
enough.

My mother fishes a small mirror out of her purse, and a
pair of tweezers. She begins plucking her eyebrows fast and
hard.

"Have you noticed that your father's nurses are getting
younger every year?" Her voice is very tight all of a sudden.

I sit very straight, afraid to say anything.

"What do you think happens to the ones who get older?"
She turns her face from side to side. Then she settles back
on the cushion.

"Mirror, mirror, on the wall. Screw the prettiest of them
all. I'm the wife."

～～～

As my father reads the newspaper at breakfast the next day,
he glances up at my mother and frowns.

"Watch that third piece of toast, babe," he cautions her.
"Do you really want that?"

"Should I, Jim?" my mother asks my brother, smiling
wide.

"Go for it, Mom." My brother moves the cereal box,
blocking the line of vision between him and my father.

"Can you pass the sugar, *dearheart*?" she asks me, still
smiling, her eyes dark and furious.

Deliberately, she dumps the whole sugar box on top of a
piece of toast. White crystals spill out over the kitchen table
and make a small mountain on the bread. She takes a huge
bite, smiling.

"Mmmmmmmmm!" she says, looking at my brother, winking.

My father gets up to go jogging, red, but very calm. He brushes the spilled sugar into a newspaper, rolls it up, and deposits it in the trash can. He kisses me lightly and swoops for my brother, but Jim turns his head away.

My mother watches him with binoculars as he jogs down the beach.

"We're not going to let him get away easy," she says to Jim.

⌒⌒⌒

My mother doesn't make friends easily. She says women are naturally sneaky, plus they're also jealous liars. She doesn't talk much to Mrs. Miller or any of the other tennis ladies, because she says every woman in Palos Verdes is after my father. It's true that my father winks at Mrs. Miller when we see her at the park. Sometimes he looks at a girl walking down the street so hard he almost crashes the car. He assures me it's normal to look at pretty women, the way you look at nice sunsets and beautiful paintings. I tell him he should look at sunsets, not at Mrs. Miller, if he wants to stop fighting with my mother.

Tonight we're celebrating my father's birthday at the Beach House Restaurant, when my father makes a joke with the waitress.

"How come a nose isn't twelve inches long? Because then it would be a foot."

The black-haired waitress likes the joke a lot. She laughs for a long time and tells him he's a real cut-up. After watching my father watch the waitress sashay away in her short black skirt, my mother takes the car keys, excuses herself icily, and throws them off the balcony into the ocean below.

I don't dare laugh. Still, it's funny to see my father in the middle of a busy street, wearing his nice tweed suit, yelling at my mother's taxi as it pulls away.

~~~~~~~~~

When my father comes home, my mother is packing.

"This place is full of crazy people, Phil. Homewreckers. Surfers. Loons," she says while she folds neat stacks of nightgowns into a black leather suitcase. "Jim's friend Aaron saw you at lunch with *her*. You know who I mean."

"Which *her*?" My father laughs. Then he says that he often lunches with his nurses, "or pharmaceutical saleswomen, or female staff members."

"Or young, attractive tennis ladies," my mother adds slowly. She looks up for a moment. "By the way, we spoke with a lawyer, we can sue you for humiliation," she says, folding. Then she looks at my brother. "Tell him, Jim."

Jim opens his mouth, but doesn't say anything. My mother looks at him, eyes pleading.

I jump in. "He doesn't want to, Mom's making him."

My mother keeps folding, furious. "Yes, he does."

"Hey, sport, do you really want to go with your mother?" my father asks Jim. "What if you end up in a place with no waves?"

"Why don't *you* leave, Dad," Jim says. "Go chase some tennis skirts."

After a long silence, my mother laughs.

My father steps forward, slapping Jim's face. A cracking sound reverberates through the room. Jim turns to my mother in shock, touching his face. A current passes between them.

Almost as if it were an old-fashioned silent film, my brother draws his right arm backward, hurls it forward, and punches my father full in the mouth. When my father goes down, my mother gasps. My father's sunglasses fly out of his pocket and land on the tile with a crunch. They spin in the silence, until they clatter to a dead stop.

My mother stands absolutely still, her arms at her sides, looking at my father crouched on the floor, covering his head with his arms. Then she crosses over, standing directly above my father, staring down at him.

"Okay now," she says. Her voice is rich and soft. My father is still crouched low, as if in the middle of an earthquake drill.

He looks at my mother as if she were very far away. My mother purses her lips and nods again, then whispers something in Jim's ear. He leaves the room, dead white, robotic.

My father stays on the floor.

My mother stands over him, a small smile on her face. She says Jim is going to protect her from now on.

"That's the last time you'll humiliate me, Phil."

✆✆✆

Later I spy on my father as he's packing his things to move to a motel. A purple bruise has begun to spread under his mouth like sloppy clown makeup. My mother sits in the bedroom on the suitcase, looking calmly at him.

"If you go to the police I'll say he was defending me."

"I don't blame Jim for this, Sandy."

My mother stares triumphantly at my father before she goes on.

"Things are going to change now."

"Okay, Sandy," my father says tiredly. "Truce? For Jim's sake?"

As she smiles at him, a ship's light disappears on the ocean.

∽∽∽

The sand rises up on a crest in the middle of P.V. beach, making a throne for the popular kids. Everyone else sits in the furrows and cracks along the cliffs.

The girls of Palos Verdes sit around in little groups. The towel girls, the Jews, the Chinese girls, the softball players. Each is a clique of seven to fifteen members who sit together in designated areas and talk only to each other. The members of each group dress alike. They wear the same lipstick colors and have similar bathing suits. Their parents have roughly the same amount of money.

The ones you notice are the towel girls, beautiful creatures who lie on Bill Blass towels, developing dark tans, sitting in their own circle on the high sand, reading fashion magazines with dark Vuarnet sunglasses perched on their upturned noses. They arch their perfect brown backs and adjust their pearls while they wait for their boyfriends to reemerge from the water. Showing the boyfriends how lucky they are.

The towel girls affect terribly bored facial expressions and eat chilled apple slices out of delicate Japanese coolers. They also keep beer cold in these coolers, beer for the boys who gesture for it later, after a few sets of waves. The girls learn from their mothers, towel mothers who pour perfectly chilled martinis for their husbands after a hard day at work. They learn serving and pouring early.

There are only a few ways to greet the towel girls. You can walk quickly past them, holding up an index finger as if testing the wind. Or you can nod your head in their general direction without nodding to any specific girl as a mark.

Nothing that insinuates friendship with a towel girl is acceptable, such as walking clear into the middle of their group and saying, "Hi, Heidi, what's up?"

If this etiquette is breached, if you dare address one of these girls in person, she will lean over to her friends, giggle prettily, and say, "Oh my God! Did you hear something?"

～～～

A few weeks after the big fight, my father comes home from the motel. He sleeps in the guest room now. I'm the only one who talks to him at breakfast; my mother whispers with Jim, all the while slicing mangos, pouring juice, pulling her hands through her cheerful hairstyle. But she glowers silently when my father suddenly gets up from the table without eating.

"I'm going for a morning set with the Mad Servers at the tennis club," he says.

"Keep your eye on the ball," my mother says, looking at him.

～～～

Usually she makes black-pen lists in the morning. Things to do. Things to buy. School schedules. Lesson schedules. Car pool. Today she makes a red-pen list, taping it to the refrigerator, where my father can see it.

Sandy's Day

1. Phil's laundry.
2. Phil's bills.
3. Phil's mess.
4. Phil's bullshit.
5. Family meeting at 6:30.

At our family meeting she says she's no longer going to be fake. She announces that the ladies of Palos Verdes can take their perfect lives and shove them up their asses.

"No tennis clothes. No Lancôme Hydrate. No Perfect Rose lipstick."

She won't cook balanced meals. She'll sleep all damn day if she feels like it. She'll eat like it's going out of style, as many cookies and chips as she likes.

She tells my father there's only one way she'll stop eating—we have to move to a small town she just saw on a TV movie, Blaine, Minnesota, where the women don't wear tennis skirts, and my father won't be faced with so much temptation from tennis ladies.

"It's the land of ten thousand lakes," she says dreamily.

"But you don't even like water," I say.

༄ ༄ ༄

Surfing is many things. Sometimes it's a religious experience, sometimes pure domination. I tame a patch of milky waves, ride on them as if they were beautiful horses. The girls taunt me at school, chanting, *"Fatty Mom. Elephant*

Mom. Big as a whale. Gross as a snail." But in the water, they can't reach me.

I love stepping into my wetsuit, tightening the zipper slowly up my back, feeling my naked skin against rubber. As I begin to paddle, long strands of wet hair tickle my neck, cashmere soft in the salty water, making me shiver and giggle out loud. Sometimes I lie in the sun for a few moments, hair fanning out, face to the sky, feeling exotic and beautiful.

It's a frank sexual pleasure to be wet and warm, lying alone on my stomach near the mouth of the sea, relaxing completely, then pushing my body upward while taming the liquid motion.

After school, I love to be in the safe, warm curl of a tube.

〜〜〜

The winter surf is kicking up. Mountains of water are moving toward our house, carrying more and more abalone shells to the beach. There is a storm off Mexico, Hurricane Alex; the waves are five feet high.

Jim and I have been surfing for nearly seven months, but we've never tried waves bigger than three and a half feet. We huddle together in the yard, deliberating. Jim says we should tell Skeezer we're sick.

"Both of us?" I ask. "They'll never believe it. They'll say we're scared."

"We'll say you gave me the flu. I feel sick, I swear."

We take our boards to the pool and lay them belly down in the blue, calm water. For a while, we paddle from end to end, discussing different kinds of flu and their symptoms. There's the Chinese kind that makes you barf for seven days and the Taiwanese kind that gives you the runs. Jim says we can pull off the Taiwanese kind if we take six Ex-Lax pills each.

"Ex-Lax is disgusting," I say. "Besides, we're good enough to go out now."

I remind him that he never falls off. "You're just afraid the older guys will laugh and call you a grommet-fag."

"Maybe," Jim admits, picking at his fingers. "So what?"

Then I thrash around in the water, making the biggest waves I can, and tell Jim to stand up. He stands up, and laughs.

"See, you're not gonna die," I say, and I slap him a high five.

We suit up on top of the cliff stairs. I rub Jim's back before I pull up the big zipper in the back of his wetsuit. By mistake I catch a piece of his skin in the fold. I put my hand over my mouth, sucking in my breath.

"Oh my God," I say, "I'm sorry."

"What?" he says absently, leaning out to look at the waves. Then, "Damn, I don't think I can do it."

I tell him my secret strategy. "Pretend you're a barnacle on the back of a whale—stuck on forever. Pretend there's no way the water can throw you."

He shrugs, telling me to forget it. "You always imagine crazy stuff. When I get scared, my mind goes blank and I don't even know what I'm doing."

We smoke an entire joint on the way down. But Jim lights another one at the bottom.

"Forget it," he says when we get to the rocks. Looking at the towers of water, he stands still and white, holding his board stiff, like a wax statue.

I push him toward the water.

"You're gonna rule the waves," I say.

A few of the guys are watching us. Jim gives them the thumbs-up. When he turns, his eyes are raging.

"Stop poking at me!" he says. "Don't treat me like a baby in front of everyone."

The waves are a translucent emerald green, highlighted by sparks of light thrown by the setting sun. I've been paddling for fifteen minutes, but I haven't reached the wave-break yet.

The waves are far more powerful than I thought. I can hear stones and heavy shells rumbling against the bottom.

First I try to go around the break, through to the left, but the current is too forceful, so I throw my board down and fight the whitewash in front of me. My arms are heavy with fatigue, and I'm swallowing mouthful after mouthful of spray. I can't see the sets that are coming because my eyes are slitted against the sting of salt. Finally there's a small lull, and I paddle.

Jim is nearly out. He jumped in at the jetty and started stroking, smooth and fast, riding up and over the wave faces, his powerful shoulders pushing him much quicker than I could follow. At first he tries to wait for me, but I motion him to go ahead. Now I see him with the guys, lined up, ready to go for a turn, astride his board with his legs deep in the water.

I see Skeezer being spit forward. He dances from right to left, swaying before gaining balance, leaning forward then lurching to the left, perfect. Another set comes. Another lull.

I paddle ferociously and make a lot of ground. I'm almost there, ten feet away, when the next set comes. Aaron lines up, ready to go, but I see my chance. I scream "Mine! Mine!" and turn around to catch the swell. It's late, already breaking when I catch it. The wave throws me sideways, but I hang on, stand up, and whip around in the force. Hair slaps over my eyes so I'm blinded. The roar of the water comes down as I slide over the wave, fishtailing back and forth like a sewing needle gone awry. Somehow I stay up, leaning forward, almost retching, ready to fall. But suddenly I'm riding instead, falling from the sky, watching the horizon surge upward. Then I'm kicking out just before the tube closes. I get slapped by the next wave, and the next. I'm holding on to my board with one hand, dog paddling with my other, turning my face away as the current pushes me back and forth.

"I got it," I yell to the guys. *"I got a wave."* I paddle close to Jim in the next lull. Everyone is amped. Skeezer smiles at me. Tad gives me the thumbs-up.

"Hey, don't snake any more waves, Medina," Aaron says. "There's a fucking lineup, you know."

"Give spaghetti arms a break," Skeezer calls out. "It took her long enough to find us out here."

Jim joins in. "Yeah, mellow out."

He smiles at me and takes off on the next wave. All I can see is his muscled back, almost black in the semi-darkness. He stands straight, tall, maneuvering back and forth, graceful and powerful. His hands are low at his side, his left foot barely raised.

When he kicks out, the board flows sweet and steady, spinning in the water overhead. Even when he goes under, he's smooth, controlled. He comes up laughing, holding his arm up in the air in triumph. He swims right up next to me, and winks, telling me how perfect I was.

Walking home later, Jim kicks the dead brush aside for me. He doesn't say much, but he comes to my room later to say goodnight.

"Goodnight yourself," I say, grinning.

He hangs around for a while, picking through my records and magazines, then he sits down on the floor, putting his big, smelly feet up on the bed. He turns off the lamp. "That was fun today," he says in the dark, "maybe one of the most fun days I've ever had."

I nod, smiling, starting to fall asleep.

"Do you think the best times we'll ever have are happening now?" he asks softly.

"Don't think like that," I say sleepily. "It's bad luck."

⌒⌒⌒

At school they test my IQ, tell me to look at a bunch of swirls and tell them what I see. I tell them I see waves, and starfish, and whirlpools. They write words down on a pad of paper, and look at each other, nodding. They put me in with all the smart kids in a class track called Mentally Gifted Minors.

My father says I'm a lucky girl to get into this program.

"Nobody likes a brainbox," I say.

But brainbox classes are okay. Cami Miller isn't in MGM, so she can't tease me, or hold me down and spit in my face, or tell me I'm ugly and a total freak. Plus, the brainboxes don't joke about my mother; they don't care about anything except fractions and trigonometry and Harvard and Yale.

Jim isn't in any of my classes. He gets stoned before the swirl test. He goes with a few of the other surfers, tells the tall lady he just sees a bunch of black shit on a page.

They put him with all the popular kids in remedial math, woodshop, metalshop. He smokes pot with them, makes jokes, laughs. He's the lucky one.

❦❦❦

Some of the Bayboys tease me about my flat chest and skinny neck, but a few of them are pretty nice. Once when I step on a sea urchin, Charlie Becker, an eighteen-year-old, helps me pull the slender spines out of my feet. I pretend it doesn't hurt, even when he digs around with a needle to find the broken-off pieces of the quills. As he dips my foot in water to clean off the blood, he tells me to wear surf booties next time—watertight slippers made of thick rubber.

"You'll have better grip; they stick really good to surfwax. And the urchins won't get you as bad."

Then he tells me to keep it up, to forget what the guys say.

"I've been watching you out there. I think you could get pretty good, *if* you get serious about it."

Then he laughs and tells me I better practice a lot, because perfect balance takes years to attain.

The next day I go to Mrs. Ornage's house, the old French piano teacher, and tell her I've decided to surf more, so I won't be coming to any more lessons. She sits with her back very straight, playing a small song on the piano, smiling faintly.

"Yes," she says, "maybe you will be better at this surfing than you are in piano. It is important to do something that you are good at."

That week I also quit flute and tennis.

❦❦❦

My father doesn't spend much time at the house anymore. Even on weekends he plays tennis, then goes to the hospital to catch up on paperwork. On weekdays he works later and later. One day my mother corners him as he leaves, smelling of cedar soap, carrying a tennis bag and a change of clothes. My mother turns to Jim, laughing and whispering, like one of the girls at school.

"Your father is playing a lot of tennis these days. They say he has a great *serve,* and a good *lob.*"

Jim stays quiet, not sure what she means. My father sighs.

"Sandy, we have a truce, remember?"

My mother pushes. "We're moving to Blaine, remember? That was my deal."

My father stands his ground. He avoids looking at Jim; his answer is very slow and precise. "I can't move to rural Minnesota, I have a good job here."

My mother's eyes are grim, but she smiles. "Well, Jim, it might be you and me then," she tells my brother, looking at my father. "You'll come with me, won't you?"

Jim looks out the window, nods his head.

I stay up late, tossing and turning, unable to sleep. Then I go to Jim's room, wake him up. I ask him if he'd really go to Minnesota.

"We're not really moving," he says, letting me climb in. "We just have to let Dad know I'm on her side."

"How come you hate Dad so much?" I say. "He sure wishes you didn't."

Jim says my father is really bad news, he's sneaky, and he hurts my mother's feelings for no reason. "Mom's told me a lot of things about him," he says. "Really bad things."

Then he whispers that my father has millions of girl-friends, my mother found evidence—the seats in his car smell like Chanel perfume and my father isn't at the hospital when she calls late at night. Plus he comes home smelling like wine and garlic.

I laugh. I tell Jim there's no way our father would have a girlfriend.

"Besides, Mom is bigger, she could hit him," I say.

"Normal women don't hit people, Medina." Then Jim looks at me. "Besides, Mom would never lie to me."

∽∽∽

Snooping around, I find a picture of my parents just before they married. They are running in the streets of downtown Chicago, a model and a young doctor. My mother smiles as she runs, dark glasses and a flash of enamel teeth. She looks stunning in a white sweater fitted close to her slim body, a set of pearls around her neck. My father wears a black cardigan along with a pair of terrible red golf pants. As they run, they touch shoulders, but their arms are free. They look contemptuously into the lens, but they are happy. They are two people entering the long run, with a wedding ring and a dream.

∽∽∽

My dad comes down to the beach while Jim and I are out. He sits on the sand, wearing a visor and tennis shorts. I wave to him from across the water, but Jim ignores him.

I try to surf extra good, but my fins keep getting stuck in the kelp bed, so my board slides out from under me. Kelp can grow a foot a day, and it can be pretty creepy to paddle through it when it's high.

Jim wipes out twice. "Dad's bringing bad luck," he says. Then he tells me he's leaving. But instead of riding straight in, he paddles all the way out and across, to the public cliff stairs, half a mile from our house.

My father watches him go, looking very small, scooping up handfuls of sand and letting them run through his fingers.

After a few more waves, I ride in and sit next to my father. I tell him I don't usually surf so badly; I explain about kelp, how hard it is to paddle through. My father nods, tracing a circle in the sand with his toe. He asks why Jim won't talk to him anymore. I fib a little, telling him Jim didn't want to come in through the kelp bed, so he paddled farther to avoid it.

In the orange smoggy air, I see flecks of sand stuck to the wet tracks on my father's face just under his sunglasses. I've never seen him cry before.

My father puts his arms around me. He tells me kelp is good because it makes most of the oxygen in the world. I nod, feeling very sad.

"See," he says, his voice catching a little. "There're a few things I know."

Then I ask him why he and my mother fight so much.

"There're a lot of things I don't know," he says.

～～～

"Look at your famous father," my mother says, showing us a profile of my father in the *Palos Verdes Gazette.* He is wearing crisp surgeon's greens, sitting on a white hospital cot, looking at an X ray of a woman's chest. A blond nurse hovers over him, three orderlies flank his left side like soldiers.

My mother says she'd like to tell the real truth to the newspapers. "He doesn't fix hearts, he ruins them."

In fact, my father never ruins anything. He has fixed a lot of hearts. Famous hearts.

While he's at the hospital, my brother and I like to look at his books. We sneak into his office, and open to page 223—a naked lady page—Jim's favorite.

The patient is lying on the operating table. Her breasts are visible, covered with a transparent greenish sheet. But it's her heart we are supposed to be looking at. A heart that has *arrhythmia mita extremis,* a rare congenital disease.

There are three doctors over her with thin, silver knives. One of the doctors has big, bushy eyebrows. This is my father. He is repairing a "collapsed left artery," the text says, "with the expert concentration of a master surgeon."

But my brother isn't interested in this. He looks at the lady's breasts and laughs.

"You're so gross," I tell him. "That lady is sick."

"Dad's the one who's gross. He's the one who does it."

"He's looking at her heart," I say. "He doesn't care about those."

Except, in the picture, my father isn't looking at her heart, exactly. He's looking at the camera and smiling.

～～～

"I thought you might want to look through this catalog, Sandy. There's so many things you could be good at." My father is eating breakfast with us for the first time this week. His words sound stiff, rehearsed.

My mother smiles as she looks at the course titles my father has circled in the community-college handbook: *Art History: The Impressionists from Seurat to Van Gogh,* or *Yoga,*

Find Inner Peace!, or the one she laughs at, *Summer Gardens: What You Should Know About Drought Tolerance.*

"I already know about drought tolerance, Phil," she says.

෨෨෨

There's a lot of things you have to know if you don't want to be x'd out with the Bayboys. Your hair has to be a plain crewcut, or long and feathered like Skeezer's. You have to wear tan or black boardshorts, the extra-large kind that come to your knees. I wear boy's boardshorts, because most girl's bathing suits are weird, either too lacy or very skimpy. Some of the guys think it's funny that I wear trunks.

One time Andy Aaron is reading *Surfer* magazine at the cliffs, when he holds up a full-page ad of a busty girl in a bikini kneeling on the sand.

"How about them apples," he says, waving the magazine around, howling like a dog. Suddenly the rest of the guys are howling, too, panting and beating their chests like gorillas.

Skeezer calls out to me, "Hey, Medina, why don't you ever wear a bikini like that?"

Blood rises to my face, but I laugh and pretend to go along with the joke. He asks again, walking over to me, "Why not, Medina? A nice yellow string bikini?"

"Bikinis are stupid," I say. "Besides, it would fall down in the first big wave."

"It would fall down anyway," Skeezer says, running his hand up and down in front of my chest, indicating a flat board.

When I don't say anything, he draws up his shoulders and smirks.

"Oh, you'd look all right in a bikini." He slaps me on the back. "Don't be so sensitive."

I smile but don't look at him. Later I cut him off and snare his beautiful ride on a good three-footer.

"Don't be so sensitive," I say when he shakes his fist at me.

But it's not just hair and swim trunks, there're other unspoken rules. P.V. surfers never wear colored wet suits, or anything bright or modern, no neon. They only wear black wet suits, holes patched with duct tape, discolored with resin stains. They have one- or two-fin boards. They don't ride squirrelly, stupid, tricky tri-fins, and don't like anyone who does.

Secretly, I don't care that much what anyone wears. I don't even care if they surf in sopping wet Levis like some Vals do. For me, the only thing that's sad is watching people go to work in their suits and ties.

It feels so great to walk away and go surfing.

∽∽∽

My mother is reading a book by a famous TV psychologist who says most of a person's personality traits are in their genes when they're born. She tells Jim I was born with the same sneaky gene that my father has, that's why we're in cahoots, ganging up against her all the time.

"Mom says you and Dad are alike," Jim says thoughtfully. "She knows you have secrets with him."

I tell him it isn't true. My stomach twists around, the way it always does when Jim gets nervous about me.

"No women like you. The towel girls hate you, too."

"They shouldn't," I say. "I don't even talk to them."

"That's just it. You don't talk to anyone but me. You go around giving people creepy stares all the time."

I tell him I don't feel comfortable around anyone but him.

He sighs. "I just want you to be normal. I'm tired of defending you to everyone." Then he tells me to forget it, I wouldn't understand.

Even though I offer to give him my new *Surfer* magazine, he doesn't respond.

Instead he says he wishes I were different, sometimes.

My brother and I are in my parents' bathroom brushing our teeth, because our own sink is stopped up with dog shampoo and fur. Jim is in a really bad mood because my mother was crying all night, and he had to go sleep in her room. Quickly he rifles through my father's rows and rows of vitamins.

"I dare you to take these," he says, pouring out nine bright pink capsules of niacin into his hand.

"What are they?" I ask suspiciously.

"Just vitamins, from Dad's shelf."

"If they were just vitamins, you wouldn't be laughing," I say.

"Don't be a pussy, just swallow them, they aren't gonna kill you."

"If it hurts, I'll kick your ass," I say.

"Oh, you will?" He is punching me, knocking the wind out of me, bending over my face like a hippo. "Kick it then, kick my ass, big mouth," he says.

I lie on the tile stunned, trying to breathe. He leans in close, looking very strange, angrily pushing the pills in my face.

"Go on, tough girl, or are you scared?" He flaps his arms like a chicken's wings, clucking, "Bok bok bok." His eyes are bugged out, sweaty hair stuck to his forehead.

I grab the pills from his hand and swallow them, my eyes closed.

Within minutes my face is flushed bright red, my palms and feet are itching like crazy, my heart is pounding too fast. I am gasping for air. "How come you made me do that, Jim? I thought we were best friends."

"Oh, man," my brother says, dropping down next to me, hugging me. "I'm sorry. I'm so sorry."

And then I'm comforting him, trying to stop him from bashing his head against the floor.

こうしてこう

Orky and Corky are trained whales at Marineland, the big sea aquarium near our house. Orky knows how to do back flips and dance to the Donna Summer song called "I Feel Love." They are both very talented and famous. They've been on TV at least six times.

But one day Cami Miller pins me down after class and calls my mother *Orky*. I try to stay calm, but she keeps pinching at me, telling me how ugly I am. I punch her in the side of the jaw until she cries. I say, "I dare you to say that again."

"Orky, Orky, fat as a whale, gross as a snail," Cami says, scratching at me. I punch her hard in the stomach. "Your mother is so gross," she says, "such a whale." I pull her hair until it comes away in my hand, and then shove it in her gagging mouth. The principal suspends both of us from school for three days.

My father comes to my room and says, "I'm going to have to ground you this time. Your mother's very upset."

I tell him how everyone at school makes fun of her, I tell him they call her Orky and make whale noises at me when I walk through the halls. My father turns very red. A vein pops out, pulsating on his neck.

"From now on, Medina, if the kids call your mother Orky, just pop them one in the nose for me."

I start to laugh and say, "That's what I did. I got suspended."

"You've got to be smarter next time," he says. "Wait until after school."

After school the sky is white. The air crackles like hot paper. The annual heat wave came early, in the middle of winter, just before the big waves started to hit. I'm still grounded from surfing.

I'm hosing off my surfboard, talking to the ancient Japanese gardener as he soaks the dying spider orchids with a watering can. When my board is clean and cool, I begin to wax it, explaining how to stroke it from one end to the other with a bar of coconut oil so it leaves behind a small residue of film.

"That way you don't slip off when it's wet," I tell him.

The gardener smiles, uncomprehending, wiping small beads of sweat from his brow with a handkerchief. He nods his head as he kneels in the bush, ripping away parched leaves with his fingers.

I'm sharing with him in detail all the different kinds of surf wax—the kinds made with pure coconut and the inferior kinds cut with animal fat. I put the board to his nose and he laughs and says, "No, no . . . busy right now."

I push. "Come on, it's just coconut. Just smell it a little."

There is a tap at the window. A rap, klonck, klonck, and a voice that is girlish and sweet.

"Medinaaa," my mother calls, "I want you to come in now. Nooow." She wiggles her fingers at me and then pounds three times on the glass.

She is in her bedroom when I go inside to face her. There is a note on the kitchen table that warns me "not to parade around half-naked in front of the gardener." The house is quiet. I smell bacon and anger in the fading light.

⌒⌒⌒

At 1:30 A.M., my mother comes to my bedroom, shaking me awake from a deep sleep, holding a pair of nylon shorts between her fingers.

My mother holds my face, cradling it, and rubs the nylon between her fingers, close to the small of my ear. It makes a scratchy noise, a dry itchy noise, sending off sparks from the heat.

"These shorts are not what an old man should see. I saw him. I saw him looking at you."

As I try to wrestle my face from her hands, she tightens her grip.

"You think you know about men just because you've charmed your father, but you don't."

Then she wipes her sweaty fingers on her white night-gown, dropping the shorts in the hamper without another word. She slams the door to the bedroom with great force. She uses the door as a form of communication, as a punctuation mark.

I will never wear Dolfin shorts again. I will wear only striped shirts, beige sweaters, huge taped-up chino pants. Cami says only lesbians wear chinos, so maybe I'm a dyke. All the girls circle me after school, whispering, *"Weirdo, dyke."* Then they try to make me kiss fat Dina Hauser, holding me down on the grass, pressing my face against hers.

I fight them until the principal comes, but Dina rolls over, plays dead. Her eyes are calm, resigned.

Jim tries to throw my chinos over Gull Cliff the next day, balling them into an angry knot, hurling them as far as he can.

But I gather them up again. I run down the sheer face of the cliff, scooting like a crab, using both my arms and legs, triumphantly bringing up the pants on a broom handle.

I laugh, shaking the dirty cuffs in his face like a witch doctor.

I tell him never to do it again. I tell him I love these clothes of my father's more than almost anything else. "Except not more than you, Jim, you idiot."

"I love you, too, you bitch," he says, but he's laughing.

The next day I'm running very fast with my father. The harder I run, the better I feel. We run neck and neck with the greenery, the flowers. We pass blond, emaciated women, jogging and frowning, wearing pastel shorts, the thin nylon kind, and matching Nike tennis shoes, running uphill in thin files.

My father keeps looking at his watch because fat begins to burn after twenty-two minutes. The rest is only water loss.

My father barely sweats. He wears aviator sunglasses like a movie star.

"Looking good," the women call out.

Later we sit at Palos Verdes Park, stretching out after the run.

Still breathing heavily, he asks me, "What would you think if I moved out for a while?"

I close my eyes and stretch very hard, feeling pain radiate down my calf to my foot.

"I think that would be very bad."

He exhales, explaining that things have gotten to "the point of no return" at home. He says my mother will be much happier without him in the long run.

I bend all the way over, pulling my torso toward the ground. The muscles constrict and tighten down my back. I force my head all the way between my knees and keep it there.

"Why don't we come live with you?" I ask him, the words half-garbled, my throat constricted.

My father sits down on the grass. He puts his chin in his hands. "That wouldn't be practical, princess." Then he tells me the real truth, that he's fallen in love with someone else—someone he's very serious about. He says it happened by surprise, that he hopes I'll understand he's getting a second chance to be happy now.

All of a sudden, blood is rushing to my ears. I can't hear what else he says, I feel like I'm going to pass out. His mouth is still moving as I straighten up. I see him reach out his hand to me, but I don't take it.

"Jim told me about all your girlfriends," I say. "I didn't believe him."

I tell my father not to hug me. "I'm not a baby anymore."
But I cry like one anyway.

❦❦❦

My mother always cries into a pink tissue when she's planning revenge. Today she's looking out the window at Skip
Dreeter, a twenty-year-old surfer. His legs are muscled, his
hair bleached, his skin broiled bronze, his teeth cold and
white.

"Like a good string of pearls," she murmurs.

I spy on her through the hall stairs as she watches old Skip
and his friends surfing in front of our house. Her breath
comes quickly, like a terrier's.

"Maybe I'll do it, too," she says. "My God, he's beautiful. Look at him."

Skip comes forth, under the window, tossing a laugh over
his shoulder, riding a sudden wave, then dropping into the
skin of moving water. My mother touches her face with the
tissue, a deep flush comes over her. She leans closer, over
the mirrored coffee table, panting a bit with exertion. She
starts to stand up.

Then she sees her reflection in the mirror. The puff of buttery jowl that has just begun to form, the cruel rings of her
neck like a freshly cut cake. She notices my shadow. "Hey,
sneak," she says, not looking at me.

"The beautiful part is over."

❦❦❦

Most of my father is gone when I come home from school. His suits, books, ties, cologne, and toothbrush have vanished. His body has been cut, not carefully, from all the family photographs. Sometimes a hand or the crook of an elbow remains, a strange void of empty space surrounding it.

My mother can't bring herself to cut the expensive oil painting of our family above the mantel. Instead she tapes up a piece of black velvet, leaving a black space between my brother and me, covering our father completely.

At first, I peek every day behind the velvet to see his smile. Jim never does.

∽∽∽

"Men only want what they can lift." My mother is weighing herself. "Your father used to be able to lift me."

I look at my mother's nude body in the fluorescent light, embarrassed at the size of her nipples. Her nipples are burnt orange–colored and larger than teacups. Her nightgown is hanging on the hooks of the shower door, food stains around its lacy neckline.

"He's the one that made me do this," she says, grabbing flesh in her hands. "When I married him I was one hundred twenty-five pounds exactly."

Then she tells me to come to the kitchen. She takes a Hefty bag out of the pantry and fills it with five packages of frozen meat from the freezer. She hands it to me to hold.

"This is only half as much I've gained since I married him," she says.

I put it down on the floor and try to sneak out, but she

tells me to come back, or I'm grounded from surfing. "Pick it up, girl," she tells me.

I hold the meat, switching the weight from leg to leg.

"Sixty pounds, almost," she says.

When it starts to defrost, she puts it back into the freezer.

When I look out the window, I see the whales going by.

⌒⌒⌒

My mother says Jim is the new man of the house. She increases his allowance by twenty dollars a week, plus he gets tea with sugar and freshly baked cookies with cocoa sprinkles. My mother says the man of the house has extra responsibilities, so he gets special privileges.

"Oh, you're so special," I tell Jim, "but if you sit around here, you'll miss all the good waves."

He goes to the window, watching a wave scoop up Skeezer and Mikey. His breathing is even, he stares transfixed. My mother waves her hands in front of his eyes.

"Hello—earth to Jim," she says brightly. "The last thing I need is for you to get *sad* on me!"

Then she tells us we're going to start a new life. No health foods, no running. Nothing bad anymore.

She offers around a box of Mallomars, telling us we'll celebrate.

I sit on the kitchen counter, licking the salt off the top of saltine crackers.

"Oh, well, let your sister be a sourpuss. I guess she's watching her weight," my mother tells Jim.

"You're the one who's watching my weight," I say.

Jim sits in the middle, narrowing his eyes at me.

෴෴෴

When we go out surfing later, Jim sits on his board, barely moving. He doesn't paddle for any waves. They're just junk waves anyway, small choppy swells that bob upward and go nowhere.

I joke with Skeezer and Tom Alexander, telling them I'm gonna be the next Frieda Zane—the most famous woman surfer in the world.

"Not if you don't start getting some waves," Tom says, flicking water at me.

Later, Skeezer asks me what Jim's problem is.

"Is it a brother-sister *disagreement*? Are sissy and Jimbo spatting?"

"No. My parents are getting divorced," I say. "My dad has a new girlfriend."

No one says anything. As fog blows in, the water turns black and cold, and the other two paddle in, shouting good-byes to Jim, looking at him strangely.

Jim doesn't come close to me. He takes off on a small wave, sliding at first, looking like he's gonna wipe out, but pulling it off at the last second. He swims to the shore and gives me the middle finger over his back.

I watch the sunset alone. Big, empty clouds hang just off-shore.

෴෴෴

When my father comes to collect his family china, my mother doesn't yell at him, she even helps wrap the plates in newspaper. I spy through the door, barely breathing.

"What happened to the way it was? Why did we move here?" she asks.

"You're the one who wanted the money and the Mercedes."

"Why don't you just stop then," she says softly, "if it doesn't mean anything to you?"

He looks around, gesturing at the furniture, the bikes in the driveway, then her body.

"It isn't just the kind of thing you can stop. I think you know that, Sandy."

When they go into the bedroom and lock the door, I can barely see through the peephole. My father opens his brief-case and shows my mother a thick notebook of papers. My mother laughs at the papers; she says there isn't any reason to take things this far.

For a while, it looks as if we're all going to be okay. My mother apologizes, says my father can't leave her, he promised he'd never do it.

"For better or worse, remember, Phil?"

Then she promises she'll go on a diet, "for real this time." She'll even have her jaw wired shut like a Hollywood actress she read about, if it will make my father happy. My parents hug, both of them cry. My mother turns her face to my father like in a movie, trying to kiss him, but he jumps back, and places the briefcase on her lap, opening it. He takes her face in his hands, gently forcing her head to look at the papers.

"Here are your choices," he says.

∽∽∽

My father leaves quietly, not saying good-bye. My mother's face is puffy, her eyes bright and piercing. She acts like she's in a very good mood, laughing and clapping her hands as she tells us that my father offered to buy her a house in Minnesota, on a lake. She describes how the houses are classy in Minnesota—big porches with real antiques. "None of this fake Spanish style," she says.

Then she starts to cry. She grabs Jim's shoulders, and pulls him to her chest, hugging him tight.

"Phil promised he'd never leave me. You're all going to leave me, aren't you?"

Jim strokes her hair, murmurs softly, tells her he's nothing like our father.

"How could you even think that?" he says, pale, small.

"So you'll stay with me? Even like this?" Her voice is high, shrill, as she slaps her heavy thighs, pinches a roll of fat on her stomach, dissolves into fresh tears. Jim refuses to look at her body, trains his eyes on the flat horizon. His voice is neutral, terrible.

"Don't, Mom."

My mother suddenly stands upright, mascara running down her face, lipstick smeared across her chin, hairstyle askew. She holds Jim's hand, faces me.

"Your precious father wants to get rid of us, while he makes a new family with that woman," she snorts. "He thought he could pull a fast one on *me.*"

Rocks

✎✎✎

Jim and my mother have strategy meetings this week. She gives him my father's antique rolltop desk and a locking file box, too. After school, she teaches him about paying bills, which ones are important, which ones can wait. She also opens up a bank account in Jim's name to hide money from my father.

"If we're not smart, we could lose the house," my mother explains, sitting on a low ottoman at Jim's feet.

Jim likes sitting at my father's desk, opening the mail, drinking coffee. He's nervous about forging my father's signature on bills, though. He practices with tracing paper, looping the *P* over and over until my mother says it's just right.

When I can't stand surfing alone anymore, I ask Jim to come with me, to forget all the secret papers. He shrugs and says he can't hang around with me all the time like he used to. He has important things to do now.

"Mom needs me to help her out," he tells me. "She's been having trouble with the bank, and she needs my help fixing things." He folds his arms and talks about checking account balances.

"You don't know anything about money," I say. Then I apologize, telling him maybe I better learn, too. He shakes his head. He takes off his sunglasses, looking me in the eye.

"She heard you talking to Dad the other night. She heard you tell him she was a monster. That really made her cry."

"I didn't say anything about her." I shake my head violently, feeling a rush of cold air down my spine. "I didn't, I swear."

Jim puts his glasses back on. He picks at his nails.

"I'm not going to let you get away with talking about Mom like that," he says, leaning way back in my father's chair. "She's not tough like you are, Medina."

Later I hear my mother moving down the hall. Her steps are heavy, decisive. She stops outside my brother's room and knocks on his door.

She says she can't fall asleep. She wants him to sit with her for a while.

ᔕᓬᔕᓬ

In the morning, the guys let Jim line up first so he can get a few sets in before our mother wakes up. As soon as he sees her yellow bathrobe in the bay window, he gets out of the water to make her breakfast and bring it on a tray into her room.

All the guys stare at my mother's yellow shape pushed to the glass. They talk behind our backs one day when they think we can't hear.

"Have you checked out Mrs. Mason? Pushin' two fifty for sure."

"Fuckin' A!"

"My God, she used to be a model or somethin'. No wonder Mr. Mason left her."

"Maybe that's why Medina's so skinny. Mrs. Mason eats all the food."

After that, Jim stops surfing at all in the mornings, so my mother won't come to the window. He stays home to have breakfast with her, as much cinnamon toast as he wants, warm and sugary. Sometimes she even lets him stay home all day from school to help her.

My mother says Jim is her little man now.

"Remember how close we felt in Joshua Tree? That's how it'll be every day."

Jim makes a joke. "Can we drink beer again?"

My mother looks both ways, grins mischievously. Then she nods yes.

"Just don't tell anybody," she says, pulling an imaginary zipper across his mouth.

సౌసౌస

When Jim finally comes surfing with me, we go to a new place, P-Land, on the other side of the hill. P-Land is named after the Petersons, one of the oldest families in P.V. They used to own all the land on the north side of P.V. until they sold it to the government in the sixties. From the top of the cliff, the water's surface looks like a perfectly frosted cake, smooth ridges one after another.

Even though he won't admit it, Jim brought me to P-Land because he doesn't want my mother to watch him surf the bay. He knows she'll come to the window and the guys will stare. Lately she's been following him everywhere. Whenever he goes out to surf, she pouts and asks him how long he'll be.

At P-Land we see an old green Volkswagen bus parked in the shade of a eucalyptus. An old guy, maybe thirty-five, is smoking pot out of a four-foot water bong, waxing an old longboard. His face is brown and lined like a turtle's. His nose is scabbed over from being in the sun too much, his hair is bleached and thinning.

"That's Dan Edder," Jim whispers, nudging me excitedly, "the shaper."

Shapers make surfboards. Some of them are a little weird because they breathe in so much chemical resin and fiberglass. But they get a lot of respect. Dan is a famous shaper. He specializes in making one-of-a-kind lightweight longboards. Every surfer knows his story. He's been surfing all over the world, even to Bali and Java. He cooks hamburgers on a butane stove in his bus. He reads a lot of comic books. He takes lots and lots of LSD.

Dan lives in the bus on his parents' property, just north of P-Land. He almost never surfs the bay, except on really big days. Even then he never talks to anyone.

Jim and I paddle out, talking about Dan. Jim makes me whisper even though Dan is forty yards away.

The waves are different on this side of the hill; they break much farther out, and there's a lot of sharp rocks jutting out of the water. The water is muddy brown, filled with shells and stones that hit your arms like shrapnel as you paddle. It's hard to fight a current that wants to push your board directly into the rocks.

I try and try, but I can't line up right, so I just push off with my hands and go. I ride sloppy, dipping into the water when I grab the rails, jerking around uncontrollably, then spilling off.

Jim circles a few times, lining himself up perfectly. I watch him go as I paddle back out. He sways up and down, moving swiftly through the line of water, never even touching his rails. He's calm and cool, barely sweating as he moves up next to me again. For the first time in weeks he smiles his best, widest smile.

"Do you think Dan saw that ride?" he asks, grinning.

కానావావ

A few minutes before sunset, Dan paddles out. His arms move like spiders through the water, his face dry and calm.

"He's coming out," Jim hisses. "Be cool."

Dan paddles up right next to me, looks me up and down, and smiles.

"Hey, little thing," he says. "I like surfer girls."

He doesn't even look at Jim. But he keeps talking to me, telling me to move up on my board and paddle from the nose in rough water. He nods a lot and smiles for no reason, extra stoned.

Nothing he says makes much sense. He talks about the rat race, how you've got to get out of it and surf "free." He talks about his friend's secret pot farm in Humboldt County and a crazy dog that followed him into the water in Hawaii. He starts one story before finishing another and forgets where he left off.

I get cold listening, so I start to paddle for a wave, but Dan grabs hold of the rails of my board and shakes me around, laughing.

"Don't go anywhere, cutie," he says. "I want to talk to you for a minute."

Jim sits about six feet away, brooding now. He doesn't go for any more waves. It's dark when we get out of the water. I paddle back in with Dan, while Jim follows a few yards behind. Dan walks me up the trail. His arm keeps grabbing mine.

Just before we leave, he tells me to come back sometime and he'll show me a secret spot. I turn around and look at him, warm all of a sudden.

"What a freak," Jim mutters on the way home. Then he stays in my mother's room, watching TV, ignoring me.

❧❧❧

Even Skeezer doesn't know how to surf goofyfoot, right foot forward. That's my favorite trick, even though I'm not left-handed like most goofyfoots. I can lean way back, putting my weight on my back foot, just cruising, rubbing my stomach and patting my face, taking the top of my wet suit off, balancing it on my head.

That's what I like doing, even when they laugh at me, balancing a wet suit on my head, just cruising down the face of a wave, holding out twenty seconds, singing La-la-la-la.

Other guys get mad when there's lots of people out, but I've decided not to let crowds bother me. I'm a wave catcher. While the other guys huddle up in a pack, I go in front, first, behind, over the top; it doesn't matter. I've learned to look at surfing like a war.

The guys think of surfing as being mellow, everyone in turn, like the line at the supermarket. But I've learned to look at it like this—you only get a turn if you fight for one. I let Jim take good waves but I never let Skeezer or Mikey. Jim says if I'm not careful, someone's going to punch me, or maybe worse. But no guy in Palos Verdes would ever punch a girl.

No one has the guts to punch a Samoan either. Samoans are huge, at least three hundred fifty pounds. They have roses and barbwire tattooed on their thick necks. Skeezer says they keep guns in their wet suits.

Even if the waves are good, everyone clears out of the water when we see their battered brown station wagon pull up. We sit on the rocks, far away from the gang of Samoans as they amble down the public cliff stairs.

I've seen them reach into the tide pools and grab for fresh abalone, eating the meat from the shells raw and whole, then sucking the juices from mussels that lie clumped on the buoy. They dance and laugh together, drinking malt liquor out of brown bottles until they are so drunk that they can barely stand. I watch them from the rocks in awe. I have never seen people dance without music before.

The Samoans live in San Pedro, a city you should be afraid of. People are murdered there in their sleep for no reason.

San Pedro is twenty miles from Palos Verdes. As I ride through its streets, on the way to the mall with my father, I talk about the Samoans eating from the tide pools, sucking the fish raw from the shell. I press my hand against my father's as he quickly drives his Mercedes through the streets, decorated with graffiti, lined with barbwire.

I shiver and ask him if it's true what my mother says— that he's going to stop giving us money, so we'll be poor.

"She says you'll kick us out and we'll have to move to San Pedro and go on welfare."

"Goddammit," is all he says.

My mother is as big as a Samoan now.

⌒⌒⌒

The air is hot, humid, semitropical. I lie in a raft in the pool, rubbing my neck with an ice cube, waiting for Jim to finish talking to our mother. As I watch through the open window Jim bites his nails. My mother throws up her hands, annoyed.

"It isn't *stealing,* Jim. Your father *owes* me. *He* chose to get nasty, so I'm forced to rearrange things." She then asks if he understands the difference between stealing and rearranging.

I put my fingers in my ears, tired of hearing about money, banks, signatures, accounts. As the sun pours down, I feel more and more restless, thinking about P-Land, wondering if Dan really knows a secret spot.

I close my eyes, remembering an older guy's attention, wanting more.

⌒⌒⌒

When I get to P-Land, Dan's passed out in his bus under the old eucalyptus. But when I knock on the door, he sits up, squinting, trying to place me.

"Hey," he says, his eyes red and filmy. "Come in." He smiles, patting the stained knit afghan beside him.

His bus is dirty, strewn with sandy clothes and rusted tools. I sit on a moldy flowered cushion stolen from an old couch. I tell him I want to know about the secret spot. He rubs his hands together, looking me up and down.

"So you came for some secret fun." Then he laughs and winks, loading the bong from a Baggie stuffed with pot.

When I bend down to take a toke, he snatches the bong away, laughing, telling me I can't smoke until I meet his lady.

Then he introduces me to his bong.

"Meet Miss Lady Highness," he says, tipping the bong as if in a bow, running his wrinkled fingers up and down its neck, caressing it. "She's my best girl. I don't want her to get jealous."

The bong is yellow, cracked with age, very tall and thick like a plumbing pipe. "Miss Lady Highness" is scripted sloppily on its sides with a red marking pen. Dan lights a match to the pipe end, and tells me to suck deeply. He laughs. The pot crackles and burns, sweet in the hot air.

I smoke two deep hits, looking at him. He winks at me again; his dry, bony hand comes clamping down on my leg. I move back a little, but his hand stays locked, squeezing. The pot is very strong, the bus glows surreal orange in the sunset. Floral patterns on the pillow seem to skip and jump. His hand traverses up my leg as he tells me about a wave he surfed in Java.

"There were these electric eels underneath us, man. It was crazy!"

He puts his mouth close to my ear.

"Have you ever smoked Thai stick before, girlie?"

"Nooooo," I say, my voice very low and floating.

His hands rub rough, like a dry towel up and down my legs, leaving a trail of gooseflesh in their wake. His face hovers close to mine, expanding. He draws in a hit and exhales slowly, licking his lips, blowing hard. I put my hands in front of my eyes, waving the smoke away. I smell fish and beer on his breath as he squeezes me.

I think about how much older he is, how much respect he gets from the Bayboys. I feel good. I smile at him, wondering if he'll surf the bay with me in front of everyone. I pretend not to notice his hand.

Suddenly Dan lowers his face onto mine and pushes his tongue into my mouth, flicking it in and out like a lizard's, rough. The wrinkles around his eyes look like lacy webs up close, his lips are rough and cracked. I concentrate on keeping my mouth open as his tongue fishes around, grazing my teeth, slimy, warm. I feel his hand slip over my breast. Queer flashes of heat and light surge through the bus; I back away, gagging.

"I feel like throwing up," I say. "Are you sure this is pot?"

He gives me a shot of tequila.

"Swallow," he says.

❦❦❦

I'm kneeling over the bong, naked except for the boardshorts, drawing in another hit and another, confused, hoping to black out. When I try to stand up my head hits the quilted ceiling. I see a cascade of falling stars, shimmering silver and blue. Dan speaks, his voice hard, crystalline in the silence.

"So you *like* me," he says, giggling. "You think I'm really *keen* and *neato*." His hand locks on to my right breast, rubbing it in a circle, faster and faster, looking me in the eye. I feel nothing except the scraping of his hand dry against my skin. The water roars below, and I imagine I'm far away from the bus, taking off on a warm wave. I put my arms out as he thrusts a thin, pointed finger between my legs, jiggling it around.

"Do you like that?"

I feel his bony erection against my leg. I close my eyes, lying very still as he slides his pants off. He throws towels and clothes out of his way, laying his weight on top of me, pulling my boardshorts halfway off. They dangle, loose, around my ankles. Then he pushes into me.

"There." His eyes roll back in his head as he shudders, moaning low. He stops moving, and closes his eyes, smiling, licking his mouth. After a while, he gets up. He looks at me and winks again.

"I hope you got what you came for, girlie," he says. "Did you like your secret?"

I stare at the hollow wrinkles around his eyes, trying to focus. Warm fluid is dripping off the pillow under my back so I turn it over, wiping it carefully on the carpeted shelf.

The next thing I remember is downing two more shots of tequila, swishing it around my mouth. Then I grab a towel, run down the cliffs as fast as I can, tumbling at the steep part on the bottom. Dan comes after me, laughing, telling me I'm crazy, grabbing my legs from behind. I wade into the water, scrubbing my legs with clumps of seaweed, swirling around in the water, sloughing off the mud. I tell Dan to go away, pushing him, trying to get clean.

At sunrise, I wake up groggy, looking around at the tide pools, unsure where I am. Sharp stones stick into my naked back, my hair is muddy and matted with sand. Three East-side surfers are coming down the trail, scanning the waves. Swathing the towel around me like a robe, I hide in low, thorny bushes for two hours until the surfers are gone and the sun is high and bright. When I get to the top of the trail, Dan's bus is gone. My shirt is hanging on a tree, blowing lazily in the breeze.

The surfers are still in their silver BMW. They look at me and whisper, peeling out, sending up a cloud of yellow dust. One of them throws an empty bottle of beer out the window. It misses my head by three inches.

"Groupie," they shout as the car zooms away.

∽∽∽

I tell Jim that Dan is my new boyfriend, even though I never go back to P-Land. That's what I say when I leave the house at night, but this is the truth: I go nightsurfing alone. I make lots of noise when I sneak out my sliding glass door, even banging my backpack against the grate on purpose. Sometimes Jim stands at the window and watches me. I feel his disgust, even two miles away.

I pretend I'm having so much fun that I don't miss him, and on a wave, for one delicious moment, it's true. I push off and feel myself rise. I am on top. Pleasure surges through me for a brief, fleeting moment, like an electrical current through the water.

It's scary when I fall in the dark, alone.

⌒⌒⌒

There's a new plan: I see my father on alternate Saturdays. Either he takes me to lunch or a movie, or we shop. One Saturday he cancels on short notice.

"What excuse did your hero have?" my mother asks. "Let me guess . . ."

As she ticks off women's names, I ignore her, tell Jim to gather up his gear before the beach gets too crowded. But my mother puts her hand on his shoulder.

"Saturdays are our day," she says, speaking in the little girl voice she only uses with Jim. "Just because *he* canceled on *her* doesn't make it right if you do."

An ache fills my brother's eyes as he watches our mother framed against the vastness of the ocean. I try pulling at his shirt, whispering to him.

"You're always with her now," I hiss. "Don't turn into a momma's boy."

"At least I'm not like you, Medina," he says, stung. "I have feelings. Not urges."

❧❧❧

Jim stays away from me all weekend, making a cross with his fingers, warding me off.

I pretend I'm talking to Dan on the phone, flirting, laughing, teasing. *"At the tone, the time will be six o'clock and forty seconds,"* I hear. "You're joking, Dan," I say.

Finally Jim comes to my room, tells me we better talk. I can hardly breathe as I throw my stuff into the pack. He doesn't say a word on the trail to the bay.

But in the water, Jim gives me a warning. He tells me I better stop hanging around with Dan because the Bayboys know I'm sleeping with him. He says I'll lose all their respect if they think I'm just a surf groupie.

"What would the Bayboys think about *you*," I ask, "sleeping in Mom's room, playing cards with her every night?"

He starts to answer, but only swallows. He can't find anything to say.

Neither of us look up at the window. But we know she's there, watching.

❧❧❧

Sometimes I watch myself in the mirror while I exercise. I can see I'm not beautiful. I'm skinny, bony, ugly even. I've heard Skeezer describe my face as the muzzle of a shark. My eyes are always roving incessantly from side to side. Watching. I have unsupple skin that throws the water off it, no eyelashes, limp blond hair that falls to my waist like a plastic sheet. Legs that are too long, like a skinny bird, legs that are bowed, scarred from the jetty.

I've even studied myself in a mirror against Jim's favorite photograph of my mother when she was a model. I've seen I have no chance of being beautiful. There is no soft look in my eye, no curve to my neck.

But I am built for speed.

∽∽∽

For Valentine's Day, my father sends me a bottle of green perfume. I put a dab on, lift up my wrists and smell them, feeling very sophisticated. I don't care if my brother sees me, I don't care if he sticks his finger halfway down his throat and pretends to vomit on the tile.

After I dab a little more on, Jim grabs my wrists and twists them in an Indian burn.

"That's your valentine from me," he says, flicking me on the head with his finger. Then he smiles and takes out something he's been hiding. He checks to make sure the door's locked before he shows me.

It's a whole basket of valentines—pink paper hearts and candy kisses. He even got a candy box from Heather Hunt— the prettiest girl at school. When he shows it to me, he pretends he thinks valentines are stupid.

I nod my head, telling him I'm glad I didn't get a single one.

But when I'm alone, I watch the waves and touch myself.

∽∽∽

My brother wants to meet Heather Hunt tonight on the cliffs, but he has an early curfew. I tell him to go anyway and show him how easy it is to sneak out. But we both know why it's easy for me—my mother doesn't care what time I come home.

"Do whatever you want," she says to me when she comes to my room at midnight, waking me up. "But don't be a bad influence on Jim."

"You're the good one," she tells Jim behind my back. "Thank God there's a good one."

I can tell my brother is thinking about Heather.

One night he even takes a shower and puts on his best flannel shirt, a soft green one that matches his eyes.

But something stops him from leaving. My mother holds his hand.

Tuesday night I'm under my brother's window, waking him by throwing tiny pebbles at the screen. He looks at me, up and down, my dirty clothes and sandy feet. He opens the window slightly, just enough for me to squeeze in, not giving his hand, pointing at the rip in my shirt.

"Where were you?" he asks. "What time is it?"

We both look at the clock, its numbers reading 3 A.M.

"Mom must have locked my door," I say. "Thanks for getting up."

Jim is silent for another minute. I go on.

"I was at the cliffs. You know what I was doing."

"With a guy? Someone that you *fucked*?"

We hear our mother rising, moving her bulk out of her

room. Jim panics, motioning for me to get in the closet, shutting it quietly behind me. Our mother moves past the bedroom, tiptoeing through the hall, on a quiet sneak to the refrigerator.

"Yes," I tell him, through the slats of the closet, "it was exactly like you think it was. It was beautiful. Well it was okay, sort of. It wasn't beautiful at all."

Then there is silence. Our mother returns, unwrapping a cake, crinkling its cellophane, ever so quietly shutting her door.

"Who was it, Dan?"

"Maybe it was a new one."

Jim laughs hollowly and pops each knuckle in his hand.

"Thank you," I say, clenching my fingers.

"Fuck you," my brother says, and rolls onto his belly, feigning sleep.

"Why don't you go meet Miss Heather Bigtits. I know you're thinking about her."

"You don't know what I'm thinking," he says.

⤳⤳⤳

You never know the ocean's moods, but here are some remedies for its dangers:

1. When you get stung by a jellyfish, pee immediately on the sting. The uric acid will lessen the pain.
2. A cotton undershirt worn under your wet suit will prevent nipple rash and its mass of red, painful bumps that come from the ceaseless rubbing of rubber over bare flesh.

3. Duct tape can fix anything, a ripped wet suit, a dinged board, a smashed bottle of beer, even.

4. Sea urchins lurk under the calmest water; you need to paddle out on the nose of your surfboard to avoid getting needle quills in your feet.

5. If you've snorted too much cocaine, an hour in the water will fix your sinuses. The salt flushes the nose wounds with its moist, cleansing wet.

But these are only facts.

The rest is pure magic.

⌒⌒⌒

I'm in the water, in my wet suit, drenched, looking good. My brother nods to me, stoked that I'm getting a good set. He drops back and lets me take the waves, proud that I am the only girl who surfs in Palos Verdes.

When he smiles at me as I take off, I know exactly what he's feeling. In the water, far away from my mother's watching eyes, he loves me more than anything.

But he won't walk to the trail with me at the end of the day. He tells me to go ahead, he's going to walk with the guys later. He pretends he has something else to do, a joint to smoke, a ding in his board to patch. I pretend to believe him. But I know he is ashamed of something.

"Who were you with last night?" he asks me later.

"No one. I was nightsurfing, alone."

Jim stares straight ahead. Then he looks at me.

"Mom says she saw you at the bay with Randy Marx."

"Gross! It isn't true," I say vehemently, the hair standing up on the back of my neck. "Here, I'll ask him." I stand up, ready to shout for Randy, but Jim yanks me down. He rubs a hand over his eyes. I move closer to him.

"You know I'm not a liar."

"Okay, genius," he tells me. "Miss Mentally Gifted knows everything."

"I wish you didn't believe what people say about me."

"I thought you didn't care," he answers, half smiling, "what anybody thinks."

"I don't care about other people. I care about you—the good one."

"Just 'cuz you're bad doesn't mean I'm the good one," he says.

⌒⌒⌒

For as long as I can remember, Palos Verdes surfers have been at war with the Vals. Vals are the guys from the San Fernando Valley, forty miles east of here.

Lunada Bay, *the* bay, is one of the best surf spots in Southern California. The waves are long, clean, tubed right, with no close rocks. The bay is famous, not only for its waves, but also for its exclusivity. Locals Only—no Vals—is our policy.

You can spot a Val a mile away: they have colors on their wet suits and weird haircuts, long in the back, short on the sides. They have bumper stickers on their cars, and rusty dents.

Only Vals use leashes, the wimpy rubber bungee cords that attach a board to your ankle. In P.V., if you lose your board to a wave, you swim, ashamed, after the wipeout.

You don't do tricks, or fancy stunts. You just ride waves. You ride and you don't fall off.

∽∽∽

When Vals invade, Skeezer throws rocks at them, and Jim lets the air out of their tires. All the boys circle them in the water and jeer at them, calling them "trolls, idiots," menacing them until they pack up and leave.

The police don't mind if the guys punch a few Vals out, as long as they do it fast. The citizens wink and say it's better to keep the riffraff out. No one wants tourists or Vals parked in front of the million-dollar view.

But some of the Vals are cute, and some surf like pros. If the other guys aren't around, I even talk to them sometimes. I tell them they better run when they see Skeezer, though. I tell them not to leave their radios on the rocks if they want to take them home in one piece. I tell them they better buy black wet suits and get normal haircuts. Some of them are babes.

I never kiss a Val, though; you just can't, not even the cutest ones.

Skeezer can tell I would, though.

"Val fucker, Val fucker," he taunts me.

∽∽∽

The house on Via Neve is always dirty now. My mother will not clean, and she doesn't trust maids or gardeners anymore. She made Jim fire them last week, saying, "They're all gossips and spies for the neighbors. Besides, we have to start saving our money now."

While Jim and I take turns washing the bathtub and doing the dishes my mother lies stiff on her bed, telling us my father is late with his check. She says he might never send us money again, and we'll really be poor.

"We'll have to sell the furniture," she sobs. "Even the TV."

At dinnertime I open a can of chili, but she snatches it away from me.

"Only eat half, Medina. We have to save."

My brother looks at me, slowly grinding his teeth.

He doesn't joke around as we smoke pot and pull weeds the next week. Instead he looks out at the bay. All of a sudden, he takes his board, steadies it against the pool fence, then punches it.

I try to joke with him, I tell him it might hit back. He tells me to fuck off and punches it, until my mother comes from her room. She tells him not to stop.

"Imagine it's your father's face," she says.

～～～

My brother is leading two lives. One minute he's playing Fish with my mother, next he's acting cool at the beach, swaggering like a Samoan. He acts tough, but I can tell he's getting tired. His eyes are bloodshot, and his hands are shaky sometimes. I try to surf next to him, but he pretends to be irritated, shooing me away like a dog. Still, I never leave him.

"You're too far up on the nose when you paddle out," he instructs me in front of the other guys. Then he demonstrates the best way to paddle, pushing water backward from both hands, digging into the liquid to propel himself forward. He tells me to bend my knees slightly, to sway with the motion like a skater gliding on ice.

Another time he says, "Don't call surfing a *sport,* Medina." He winks at Mikey. "It's a lifestyle."

He's learned how to roll the perfect joint, how to say "What's up brada?" in the perfect Hawaiian accent. He sits in the center of the popular boys, drinking his beer from a cooler, joking about girls and pot, ignoring me.

But he's nervous at home. He closes the blinds as soon as he gets back from school, afraid people will see him playing cards with my mother.

"Do the Bayboys talk about me behind my back?" he asks when we're alone in my room.

⁓⁓⁓

I snoop around, trying to find out what Jim and my mother do when they're alone. Tonight they're playing checkers in the dining room. Jim is at the table, face in his hand, glum, silent. My mother tells him to cheer up—she'll make banana splits later, just the way he likes them, with freshly whipped cream. She pinches the skin on his arm, wags her finger playfully.

"You're losing too much weight. Those shorts are baggy on you."

Jim stammers. He starts to tell her he's been feeling nervous lately, his friends wonder why he doesn't come out at night like he used to.

"Maybe I should hang out with them more. Just to keep the peace."

"I don't see any reason for that," my mother interrupts,

leaning toward him. "We always have so much fun together."

When Jim doesn't answer right away, she takes his hand. "Remember what you promised? That you'd never leave me alone? That was so sweet."

Jim drops his plastic piece, fumbles for it on the ground. My mother continues playing, advancing her piece carefully. Then she tells Jim he should forget about the Bayboys. She says they're rough, ignorant, ill-bred. "You're the sensitive type," she says, feeding him a butter cookie.

☙☙☙

At school, the class has to sit through Mr. Odell's vacation slides. It was Mr. Odell's lifetime dream to go to Africa on safari. He went in the summer.

In one of the pictures, Mrs. Odell is wearing brown lipstick and sweating. She stands against a row of tall black men, doing a native dance, smiling. Everyone looks crazy because Mr. Odell used the wrong type of flash, and in place of people's eyes are glowing red dots.

In honor of Mr. Odell's vacation, the whole class has to do a paper on Africa. Anything about Africa is okay.

I get a book from the school library about different tribes. For my paper, I choose the Morubu tribe of southwestern Africa, because the Morubus believe that no one born into their tribe can ever leave. Sometimes Morubu children stray from tribal ways and go to Cape Town to eat hamburgers and smoke hash. But the elders of the tribe aren't stupid. They keep everyone's soul.

The Morubu elders burn herbs and sticks, bless them

with a name, and put them in a jar. Many Morubu youth die within months after leaving for the big city.

"With no soul, you die," the elders say in explanation. "The body dies, but we keep the soul safe."

Leaving your tribe is worse than dying. This is what I write about. Mr. Odell gives me an A plus.

I show Jim my paper and tell him about the Morubus.

"It's a fucking genius paper," he says. "You write so cool."

"Maybe we're the tribe of Palos Verdes," I tell him.

"Yeah." My brother smiles. "I want ten thousand waves and no rules at all."

〜〜〜

My father's new house on the other side of Palos Verdes is like a palace. I spy on it from Angel Point while I surf, looking at its sienna tile roof, its gardens that stretch like a belt around long perimeters. A bright white gazebo stands out against the snow poppies like a pearly carcass.

My mother says there's no way my father could buy a house in three months and furnish it like that. She says he bought the house a year ago, in secret.

"I checked," she says, holding out a phone, "and you can call a Realtor if you don't believe me."

My father hasn't invited me over yet, but I've already seen the inside of the house in a magazine. It is white and sheepskinned, crystaled, vased. It has high ceilings painted with gold filigree. It has money.

I saw my father's new girlfriend in the same magazine. She has black mink hair that falls in ringlets to her shoulders, a blinding smile, dark eyes, clear, white skin. She is much more beautiful than my mother. She looks very good sitting on the couch.

Their picture appeared a week ago in the Social Climber column in the *Palos Verdes Gazette*. My father stands with her. She hangs on his arm, all teeth and eyes and hair. The caption under the photograph says, "Phil Mason and Ava Adare . . . A Match Made in Tennis Heaven!"

Even though my father lies, I still miss him. I cut all the pictures of him from the society page of the newspaper and paste them inside a scrapbook. My father wears the same beautiful smile in every one. I cut carefully, the way my father cuts fat from people's hearts. I hide my scrapbook from Jim so he won't tear it to shreds.

When I ask my father when me and Jim can come see his new house, he corrects me gently. "Jim and I, Medina, say it properly—Jim and I."

Then he tells me it will be soon, it's always *soon*. I try to believe him and imagine myself living in the great house, with the beautiful woman and the rugs.

There's a way to tell when my father's lying. He clears his throat first.

After the article comes out, tennis wives jog past our house, looking at each other's thighs and butts and whispering, "Sandy must be going off the deep end. Have you seen her lately?"

Nobody has seen my mother lately, except in the checkout counter at Ralph's or as a bright yellow shape through our enormous bay window, visible from the beach. They tell each other gravely that my mother needs help.

"Poor Phil tried everything," they assure one another.

"Just think about Sandy, and say *no* to dessert," Mrs. Anderson says, rubbing her tummy.

"There but for the grace of God go I," Mrs. Doty says, running faster.

~~~

My mother is shaking her head. Jim sweetens his voice.

"I promise I'll come back at five. Please let me surf a little, Mom."

"Sorry, Jimmy," she answers. "Today I need you to help me write a letter to my lawyer. I'm too angry to hold a pen." She stamps her feet. "He was planning this for a year at least! He bought that house six months ago; we have excellent grounds for a lawsuit."

She turns to Jim, who's quiet in the corner.

"You and I will take the bastard to the cleaners."

~~~

Later Jim is stoned on the couch. My mother sleeps next to him. I've just come back from shopping with my father. I hold up a box for Jim to see. Inside is a brand-new pair of surf trunks, one size too big, just the way Jim likes them.

"Dad got this for you," I whisper, beckoning him.

He follows me into the hall and takes the box. He shakes it gingerly like a box of salt. Then he puts it down, punts it across the room.

"He just feels guilty," Jim says.

"No, he feels sad. He wishes you would see him."

"Mom says not to talk to him."

"Of course," I say. "She wants you to hate him."

"Don't talk about her like she's evil," Jim warns. "She thinks you're on Dad's side. She doesn't trust you."

"I'm not on anyone's side."

"It would be great if all three of us were on the same side," Jim says. Then he points out all the nice things she does for me. "She does your laundry. And she makes dinner."

I try to steer the conversation back to our father's gift. Jim ignores me. He starts to walk out of the room, then flashes me a smile, smoothing things out.

"Guess who I talked to at the cliffs," he says. "Heather." He strikes a muscleman pose. "She says I'm a total babe."

"Gross," I say to him, laughing, punching his arm.

~~~

Heather has black hair like Ava Adare. Black hair is Jim's favorite. When we first came to Palos Verdes, he had a crush on our babysitter. Marnie always let us stay up late and snuck her boyfriend over. She had dark, wavy hair to her shoulders and laughed like a big horse, showing all her teeth, neighing.

Once when my parents were out to dinner, Marnie lit a joint in the backyard, smoking it with her boyfriend Dave by the pool. When they came back upstairs, she cooked a pan full of refried beans. Jim, reeking of my father's after-shave, stayed in the corner, glaring at Dave.

"Aren't the beans done yet?" Dave called out from the TV room, his feet up on the teak coffee table. "I've got the munchies so bad."

Laughing, Marnie stuck her finger in the pan to test the

beans. But the hot fat burned and she ran zigzag through the hall, trying to shake off sticky, molten beans that adhered to her finger.

Jim made Marnie an ice pack, elbowing Dave out of the way, telling him to go home. He promised not to tell my parents on her, and made me swear not to either.

My father teased Jim about Marnie later.

"She sure is a knockout," he said. "She looks just like your mother did when she was Marnie's age."

∽∽∽

Adrian Adare lives at my father's new house. He's Ava's son, just turned seventeen, drives a Mustang. This is all I know about him.

My father says he's a nice boy, someone I will like. He explains that Ava and Adrian aren't ready to meet us yet. He explains that this will happen soon, when Ava feels more secure in the relationship, not too far off, he says, as if he were speaking about a ship in the ocean.

"If that guy ever comes near the bay, he's gonna get it really bad," Jim says.

∽∽∽

But it's Jim who's getting it really bad.

That week he gets sick. There's a weird smell in his bedroom. I bring in the small portable television, turn it on to the cartoons, and talk to him.

"Look, it's a bird, it's a plane, it's Superman," I say, trying to make Jim laugh. I talk like Elmer Fudd, or Bugs

Bunny, and give him a running commentary about what's happening on TV.

"Now Bugs is putting a bomb shaped like a hat onto Elmer's head. . . . Now Elmer is shooting Bugs with a giant cannon. . . ."

I get good at keeping up with the sequences. "Bugs is shaking, little beads of sweat are rolling. Elmer has a mallet; he swings—once, twice—Bugs pulls out a big gun and shoots. . . ."

After a few days, Jim's breath is really terrible. He has canker sores under his nose and lips. We take him to the hospital but the doctors can't find anything wrong with him. When he comes back, he is skinnier, and weak. I don't punch him in the arm, even as a joke. I only sit with him. I describe the ocean and give him water. My mother cries. In a few weeks Jim goes surfing again. He falls sometimes now.

As I spy from my surfboard, I see Adrian smoking, reading a book, flicking out ash in my father's white gazebo. He lights one cigarette from the ash of the other. I am impressed.

Adrian is much cuter than you'd think. His hand is moving back and forth, maneuvering the cigarette from his lips to the ground. He looks small and tense. All his clothes are black. My father hates black.

"You look like you're going to a funeral," my father says to me when I wear my favorite black cashmere sweater, even though it used to be his.

⌣⌣⌣

My brother's begun to dress very carefully. He sells his old guitar and amplifier and takes the money to the mall to go shopping. He gets two bags full of new clothes, muted polo shirts and pressed chinos. He takes his time in the bathroom, too, washing his face until it's red and shiny.

The clothes bother my mother. She doesn't like his new buzzcut either.

"Oh," she says, teasing him, "do you have a new girl-friend?"

"No," Jim says. "I just don't want everyone to say we're poor."

"Oh, come on, what's her name?" my mother presses. "Or is there more than one?"

"I'm not Dad," Jim says, balling tissue wrap up and an-grily tossing it.

"I know you're not, sweetie," my mother counters quickly.

"You have to look good here," Jim says, "if you don't want people to talk."

∽∽∽

"Change places," my mother says as my brother and I wres-tle with the ring on her finger.

We've tried soap, then water, then grease from the chicken dinner. I pull on one end against my brother on the other, but the bulge of my mother's knuckle impedes us.

My brother refuses to pull any harder.

"Let's go to the doctor, they can get it off," he says. "They even take off tumors and moles."

The ring is big. It is perfect, square cut, three carats, nice. We go to the emergency doctor's office. He refers her to a specialist. The specialist gives her finger an injection of li-docaine, right between the V of her fourth finger and pinkie. Then he cuts the ring off with a tiny diamond saw.

She sends the ring to my father, after Jim removes the diamond with a butter knife. The empty band is secured with Scotch tape to the face of the doctor's bill.

"I'm keeping the diamond," she tells us. "We might have to sell it for cash."

"If we run out of money we can pawn it," my brother says.

"Better yet, we can have it insured and *lose* it," my mother answers, looking Jim in the eye.

"Lie?" Jim asks. "Face to face?"

"A little fib," she answers. "You and I'll go fifty-fifty. Then we'll have lots of money. You could get more new clothes and the best winter wet suit."

∽∽∽

At home we eat fish sticks with mayonnaise and Oreo cookies. My mother says Jim deserves lobster, steak, and chocolate mousse pie, and he'll get it after he helps her get the insurance money. But I tell Jim he might get in trouble. My mother interrupts.

"Do you think money grows on trees?" She points at me, forking a mouthful of halibut, chewing it quickly. "Do you think it comes falling from the sky?"

She wiggles her fingers in a graceful waterfall of imaginary money.

"Money is what buys nice things," she says.

"Dad gives us nice things," I answer.

"No catfights tonight, ladies," my brother says, stepping between us.

"This isn't a catfight, Jim," my mother answers icily. "It's fair for a mother to want the best for her family."

Then she turns to me. She asks me if I have a better plan to get money.

I admit that I don't.

She frowns, looking at a point just above my breasts.

　　　　　　　⌒⌒⌒

It's hazy and yellow the next day. There are a lot of by-standers on the cliff, people from all sides of the hill, because of the Lunada Bay Whale Watching Festival.

I'm in the furrow of the cliffs at Helsa Cove, smoking pot with two Eastside guys, lying lazily against gray rocks. They're both pretty cute, and I'm flirting with them, bask-ing in their attention. They talk about different kinds of pot, all with funny names: space weed, wicked red, Maui gold. I tell them I've never seen colored pot, but I have smoked Thai stick once. They're impressed. Thai stick is the strongest pot there is, and the hardest to find.

"Maybe I could get you some," I say. There's smoke com-ing from my lips as I laugh, covering the boys' faces in a maze of mist.

After a while, the bigger guy tells the other one to split. The smaller of the boys walks away, looking back sadly at us, coughing. The haze envelops the other boy as he moves toward me, gathering me in his arms, pressing his insistent mouth on mine. Wet, smacking sounds ensue.

"So you think I'm cute?" I ask him, laughing. "You re-ally do?"

I let him put his mouth over mine, tasting the dark beer on his tongue. I feel very sophisticated, as if I'm in a movie, kissing a stranger in the daylight.

He falls into the sand, pulling me down with him, hitting my head on a jutting rock, pulling at my shirt like an insistent child. I tell him to go slower, sick all of a sudden, remembering Dan. But he runs his hand over the front of my shirt, grabbing.

"Get off me before I kick your stupid ass," I say, jumping up, aiming my surf bootie square at his groin. I'm still staggering, stoned when I get in the water.

My brother is already in the water. He will not speak to me. Even when I smash the nose of my board into his legs.

"Why can't you ever be normal?" he finally spits out. "Everyone saw you with those stoner guys. Everyone." He strikes the water with his fist, telling me what he thinks I am, tears coming and falling into the water.

"What's so bad about kissing?" I say. "You should try it sometime, if Mom'll let you."

He gives my board a shove, sending it toward the rocks.

"I hate you," he says.

That night Jim stays in his room, away from me. He makes strange noises in the dark. He smokes the pot I slip under his door, but it doesn't make him mellow. When I try to apologize to him, he sings very loud to Aerosmith and rips a newspaper into a thousand shreds.

"I don't talk to sluts," he says.

❧❧❧

All the girls love Jim. They call our house late at night and giggle into the phone, asking for him, not giving their name. I feel sick to my stomach when they giggle, but I say, very nicely, "I'm sorry, but you must have the wrong number, there is no Jill here."

Then I hang up the phone and answer it when it rings again. I hear the girl on the line say, "Medina Mason is the grossest, ugliest slut alive."

I say, "What number are you calling, please?"

He shakes his head sadly when I hang up, biting his lip, not moving. He slumps low in the seat, staring at his bitten nails.

When Heather calls, I feel guilty. Reluctantly I give him the phone. His eyes are bright, alert now, but he doesn't say much. His voice is very low. He covers the receiver with his hand, curling up. He doesn't look at my mother.

❧❧❧

On Friday night he comes out of the bathroom wearing his best chinos and a tan and blue polo shirt. He looks very handsome, his hair brushed to the side, then slicked back a little with styling mousse. His eyes are bloodshot, even though he used half a bottle of my Visine.

He tries to act like it's no big deal, but my mother gets up immediately. She circles him slowly, her face dark and impassive. She doesn't say anything.

"Well," Jim says, straightening his shoulders, walking toward the door, "I'll be back by ten."

"Have fun," I say, but the words hang in the silence.

"Where is it you said you were going?" my mother asks, coming very close to him, sniffing the air near his hair. He stands in the hall, blinking under a single beam of light from the ceiling.

"I'm going to a party at Steve's with some of the guys," he tells her.

"Who's going to be at this party?"

My brother swallows. He picks at the skin on his hands. "I don't know, Mom."

"Have fun then," she says, angry.

⌒⌒⌒

At exactly ten he walks back in the door. My mother ignores him, keeping her eyes on the television, even though she's been looking at her watch every five minutes.

"Hey, Mom," he says. "What are you watching?"

She doesn't answer. He goes and sits next to her. She still doesn't talk to him.

"Hey, come on," he says. "I'm back on time."

My mother looks at him out of the corner of her eye. Then she breaks down. She cries and cries, until her eyes are swollen almost shut. Her chest is heaving, mucus and tears run down her chin. Her hands clutch at his.

"It's okay, I was only gone for a few hours." Jim's voice is very gentle, he touches her face softly. "I have to go out sometimes," he says. "But I came back. See?"

My mother tells Jim she's lonely without him; when he leaves it reminds her that she might be alone someday, without a man in the house. Jim holds her hand gently, but repeats that he has to go out to meet his friends, have fun with them once in a while.

"Why?" my mother says, her eyes filling up again.

The next day he tells me he kissed Heather Hunt in a closet. He smiles a tight smile.

"Good for you," I say, looking away. "I have some new boyfriends, too."

∽∽∽

On Halloween I'm in the back seat of Thornton Simpson's older brother's car. Thornton switches sides, sweaty thighs moving against the leather seat, looking back and forth to see if his friends are watching from the parking lot. Jim is with Heather, alone on the cliffs.

"Why don't you calm down?" I ask. "If you're going to kiss me, just stop breathing so much."

"I'm not sure I should kiss you," he answers. "You have a bad reputation, Medina. Everyone says so." Then he says he'll do it if we go somewhere else, so his friends don't see us.

"It isn't even your car," I say hotly. "You can't even drive."

"Well, you can't even shut up for a minute, can you?" he says.

"Forget it," I say, "you take too long."

"You're such a weird girl," he says, pulling the ghoul mask back over his face.

∽∽∽

Jim locks himself in his room Monday night to talk on the phone. He pretends he doesn't hear my mother, even when she walks up and down the hall, loud, four times in a row.

But later he goes to her room to make peace. He listens to her talk about my father—all the girlfriends she suspects he's had, a nurse, a lifeguard, someone's Swedish wife. Jim listens, barely talking, until she's almost asleep.

He jumps when the phone rings at eleven.

My mother tells Heather it's rude to call so late on a school night. Then she hangs up.

"She should wait for you to call," my mother huffs, awake again.

∽∾∽∾

There are the popular beaches, show beaches, where the cool, good-looking boys surf for their girls. The California dream in wave after dizzy wave—the beaches where my brother likes to go.

These days he talks to the towel girls. They laugh at his jokes, serve him beer, stretch their bodies in front of him until he sighs. I try to get his attention by waving at him until he gives me the thumbs-up sign, but he turns away from me.

I head off to Pratt Point, my new favorite break, an ugly stretch of coast to the east of our house. Only the outcast boys come here, the boys who talk about nothing except beer and water. Some of them are old like Dan, in their thirties, already lost to time. They survive alone, attached by a cord to their boards, everything else fallen away.

These are the boys who take drugs and didn't take college exams. They are immersed in liquid thoughts, how to drink too much, how to get up. How to patch their skin when it splits on impact. They are the boys who will sell anyone drugs just for beer money, surf-wax money. Practically nothing.

People call them the bottomfeeders.

"Hey, it's Jim Mason's sister," one of them says when I walk by. "Give the Jimster my regards."

I'm surprised how well the bottomfeeders know Jim. They say he's been coming around a lot the past few months. They also say he's always slow to pay, and he never jokes around. But they assure me that the drugs he's buying aren't any big deal; he mostly gets cheap "sissy stuff like dexies and Quaaludes." No big deal.

So I look the other way as they take Jim's money, give him packets, give him local's credit.

⏤⏤⏤

Jim thinks he's the only one with secrets, but I know where things are buried. My mother's right about one thing: I'm an expert spy. I'm always snooping, prying, searching in drawers. Breaking into secret places, hidden stashes of papers, reading, culling, sorting. Quietly finding out everything they don't want me to know.

Here is a letter from my father. I read it in my closet, with a flashlight, while my mother and brother watch TV.

> *Sandy,*
>
> *Enclosed you will find a check for the children's schools, plus the water bill. Please do the sprinkling at night to save money. Please turn out the lights if you aren't using them. The house will eventually be sold, like it or not, Sandy, when the kids are gone. You have no need for such a large house. For Christ's sake, you don't even like the ocean. It would be best if you followed your heart to Minnesota. My fault is that I spoiled you. You need to learn I am a doctor, not an endless nipple, running with endless money.*
>
> *Please don't lie to the kids; revenge won't help anyone.*
>
> *Phil*

*PS. The credit cards are for emergencies
only!!!!!!!*

For revenge, my mother runs the sprinklers all day, flooding the lawn. In the arid California climate, her garden sustains ferns, orchids, lush green grasses.

In the middle of the afternoon she lets the lights blaze from every room. She leaves them to burn all night, "to keep burglars away."

She heats, air conditions, ionizes the rooms. She uses electricity as a weapon.

The refrigerator is stocked, stuffed to the point of bursting, with the richest, Frenchest, most buttery foods. Dozens of frozen dinners recline in neat rows in our freezer, plus ribs, roasts, steaks standing stiff, in hulking mounds.

"We have to keep extra in case he doesn't send a check," she says.

When my father calls, angry about the tab at Lunada Bay Market, she cries to Jim.

"He'll kick me out into the street," she weeps.

"Over my dead body," my brother tells her, calm.

⌒⌒⌒

When the Vals come to the bay today, their tires are slashed, and rocks are thrown at their retreating figures. Most of them get into their dented Volkswagens and drive away.

A few Vals waver, standing with their boards at the top of the trail. They say no one owns the P.V. cliffs—they're public property. Jim runs toward them, breathing as hard as he can. He knocks a guy's surfboard out of his hand, and throws it over the edge of the cliff. It tumbles down and

down, splitting into pieces when it hits the rocks. Jim starts
throwing punches wildly, knocking a guy down as the other
Bayboys run to back him.

"Get the fuck off our beach," Jim yells, punching a small
guy square on the jaw. Skeezer jumps in, punching, too. The
guys start to run, but Jim corners them, bearing down on
them, kicking at their retreating feet. When they dive into
their car, Jim follows it down the street, kicking it, screaming at the top of his lungs. He's still screaming when the
car is half a mile away. He's breathing hard, enraged; it
takes two Bayboys to stop him from following.

"You're a crazy man," Skeezer enthuses, looking at Jim
with new respect.

Later the Bayboys slap high fives on each other's hands,
and spin tall tales about judo and protecting P.V. from the
scum. Jim says we should beat them up bad, next time. His
eyes flash as he waves his fist at the street.

"Even the genius here could help kick their ass."

"Kick it, girl," Mikey says.

Jim and I smile at each other for a split second. Then
Skeezer says, "If she doesn't fuck them first."

Motion

My brother is teaching Heather Hunt how to surf today. The top part of her bathing suit keeps coming down as the waves hit. My brother is nervous with her, motioning for me to go away.

"How are you supposed to stand up on this thing?" Heather asks, giggling.

"Whichever way feels best," he says, trying to be suave.

"Actually, it's better if you use your right foot," I say, swimming very close to them. "I don't think you're exactly a goofyfoot or anything." I say this with as much disdain as I can muster. Heather might be pretty, but she looks like a moron on a surfboard.

"What's she talking about?" Heather whispers to Jim, tossing her soft black hair over her shoulder. She gives my brother a secret wink, and then turns away.

"Could you go over there, please?" my brother says, jerking his thumb at me, twitching his neck to the left.

When I get out of the water I'm cursing. I see someone standing there, but I walk away fast, hiding my face behind my hair. I hear footsteps behind me on the rocks and someone swatting brambles and sea oats away.

I kneel down to wax my board, pretending to ignore the person. When I finally look, it is not Skeezer or Mikey.

The guy waits for the perfect time to approach, counts slowly to ten on his fingers, and doesn't move. He watches the whales go by, then I bolt up, preparing to slide back into the water, beyond him. He runs, slipping along unsurely like a crab. He reaches me and stops.

Up close, he looks like Ichabod Crane, all limbs and Adam's apple. He is wearing a thin black shirt and dark pants. He looks scared.

I jump when he comes closer. There's an awkward silence as we perch on the same rock. Slowly he folds and unfolds his hands as if he has something to give me. I pick up my board, waiting for him to say something.

"Hi, I was wondering if maybe I could borrow some wax."

I hand him the wax, an automatic Palos Verdes gesture. "Sure, whatever."

He has no board to coat with it. He doesn't move. I break the silence, ask him where he's from, pretending I don't know. He stammers and watches a gull waft by with a fish in its beak. He turns so he is half facing me, and takes a picture from his pocket, a picture of Jim and me at Yosemite.

"Look, this is you, right?" His hand shakes. "I'm Adrian Adare. I live with your father."

I look at the picture as it drops into the rocks.

"My brother'll kill you. Get out of here."

The picture floats in the tide pool. Before I can grab it, a wave of spray comes over the photograph, covering it like a mist of tears.

Skeezer and John Lapidus sit in the water, making predictions about Adrian and me. They beckon me to swim out to them. They laugh together.

"Who was that fool," Skeezer asks, "some dickhead from the Valley?"

A wave comes up, and though I'm not first in line, I jump on it. It brings me nervously toward the shore. I fall. I angrily rise.

When I paddle back out, they call to me again.

"Who is he?"

"No one."

"What did he say to you?"

"Nothing."

"Is he your boyfriend or something? From the Valley?"

They make suggestive noises and look at one another meaningfully.

I take the next wave in, running up the trail, pants in my hand. I won't let them see me cry, not for this.

～～～

Adrian waits at the top of the cliff. He offers me a joint when I reach the top. I smoke without thanking him, dragging the sweetness deep into my lungs, fighting back tears. I tap my foot, looking indifferently into the horizon.

"Why did you come here? Did my father tell you to come?"

I kick the dirt, sending clods over the face of the cliff, not looking at him.

He blows out smoke and says, "No."

"Good," I say, "good, because that would be so lame." I look past him, listening to the wild dogs scatter in the bush.

I ask him, "Do you even surf, or are you just a poser?"

"Of course I surf," he says, laughing, smoking. Then after a silence, "So your brother wants to kill me? Is he the one with that stupid girl?"

I see my brother below, floating on the water, looking at Heather's ass, smoking a joint and putting it between her lips. I give Jim one last look from the edge of the trail, pausing for a moment, willing him to look up. But he is looking only at Heather.

"Anyway, you can't surf here," I tell Adrian. "Go to Pratt

Point. They don't care where you're from if you give them five bucks."

"How do you get to Pratt Point?" Adrian asks.

I look at the way his hands open and close. His smile.

"You'd need someone to show you," I say. Then, "Maybe I'll show you."

"How old are you?" he asks as I leave.

"Fifteen."

He looks down. "You seem a lot older."

"Like, six million years old," I say.

～～～

After school the next day, the house is quiet like a library, and my mother's bedroom door is shut and locked. Jim's surfboard is haphazardly parked in the hallway, brown dog hairs stuck to the wax.

I turn up the television really loud and open and shut the refrigerator so all the glass jars of mustard and jelly bang together like cymbals. I walk heavily from end to end of the hallway, but all I hear are angry sounds through the keyhole. I smell nachos. Finally, I bang on the door.

"Jim, Jim, are you okay? Open up. Open sesame."

I hear my mother talking about Heather. She's listing all the things that can happen, how Heather could get pregnant and force Jim to marry her. My brother protests, his voice rising against my mother's, telling her he's way too young to get married.

My mother continues as if she hasn't heard him. "I want to know if you've had sex with this Heather person."

My brother is silent, embarrassed. "I don't even like Heather that much," he says twice.

"Then there's no reason to spend so much time with her," my mother says, matter-of-factly.

～～～

At night Jim stays in the black, frayed chair, watching television with my mother, looking bored, eyes red with pot. He flexes his beautiful arms as if he is aching, staring listlessly at the commercials.

He doesn't take the phone when Heather calls, just waves his hand in the air and tells me to make an excuse. After I hang up, he puts his chin in his hand and stares out the window.

I try to make jokes with him and race him down the hall, but he just watches me run. He looks at his feet, at the phone. When I sit close to him, he moves to the other side of the couch. He tells me to go away, but I don't think love is anything like water. It doesn't slip off that easily.

～～～

I slip out of the house quietly for a secret meeting. All week I've been undecided whether I should go. Jim stays in his room, playing the same heavy metal record over and over, telling me to leave him alone.

"Fine," I say, slamming the door. "I'm not going to wait around for you."

Adrian Adare is seventeen, older than I am, and smarter. He goes to the special school for super-brainboxes in Redondo Beach, so he can take a lot of science classes, get into veterinary school. He wants to get away from Palos Verdes as soon as possible, so he always studies science books, even here at the rocks on Pratt Point.

He says he has something secret to show me, but we have to get to the deep-sea kelp beds first. We walk north for twenty minutes along the rocks, then paddle far out into the water, almost a quarter mile past the breakwall. When we finally get there he hands me a snorkel and mask. Even though it's embarrassing to wear, I put it on. He tells me to dive under and look, he'll hold my board while I go.

Enormous sea ferns sway back and forth in the current. Long green grasses grow along the bottom, anchoring stalks of kelp that reach up for the sunlight. Seals swim around in the seaweed forest, slipping through tiny spaces in a blur of speed.

Fish hide in the murk, waiting to eat other fish. Tiny, yellow eyes peek out of holes in the sand. I swim a few feet backward as an Aurelia jellyfish reaches out a tentacle to sting a silver minnow, immobilizing it before pushing it through a slit in its clear, mushroom-shaped body toward its feeding polyps.

I stay under until Adrian taps my shoulder for a turn. There are pure red sea fans and thin, graceful sand filia. There are also rusty Coke cans, pantyliners, and Evian bottles.

Adrian says fish are much cleaner than people.

✎✎✎

Jim wants forty dollars today. He says he wants to buy some new tennis shoes.

"You don't even play tennis," I say. "You just want to buy pot from the bottomfeeders."

"Well, can I have it or not?"

I tell him he can have the money if he tells me what he really wants to do with it. He answers my question with a question.

"Who's that kook faggot I saw you with?"

"He's not a faggot," I tell Jim.

"He looks like one," Jim says, flexing the fingers of his right hand so his muscles stand out. "I know a faggot when I see one."

 ᔕᔕᔕ

Cliff swallows fly back and forth over my father's gazebo, surfing over currents of wind, opening their wings to the soft ocean breezes.

I relax, hiding, lying on my surfboard in the flat, blue water. It's the perfect position for spying on Adrian. I've been thinking about him a lot.

He's in the gazebo smoking, bent like an old man over a pile of books. He doesn't look like a faggot, even in reading glasses.

All of a sudden a housekeeper yells, "Mr. Adrian . . . your mother doesn't want you to smoke!" I flatten myself against the vanilla board, trying to disappear in the thin folds of whitewash in case he looks up. But he doesn't look at me. He flips his cigarette into the mermaid fountain and lights another right away. He stares dreamily at the swallows and smiles.

I go home and call him.

"Hey bookworm," I say, nervous. "Let's go running."

I want to show him how fast I can run, plus I want to show him off. I want the towel girls to see me with a cute older guy. But Adrian tells me he hates running, and besides, he has to study all night for a science quiz.

"Why do you always study?" I ask. "It's bad for your eyes."

"Don't you want to go to college?" he asks. "You're crazy if you don't."

I tell him he's the one who's crazy, always worried about his books.

"I have to study or I'll never get out of this place," he says.

That is an answer I can understand.

❧❧❧

It's sunset. Adrian and I are sitting on the cliff in the Mustang, low in the seats, laughing as we make a list of all the people we hate.

"Cami Miller, because she's a big phony," I say. "Believe it or not, she eats piles of French fries and throws them up in the school bathroom."

Adrian laughs. He shows me a page in his natural history book about birds called great frigates who follow smaller birds around and beat their wings until the little birds get scared and throw up.

"Then the frigates eat the vomit," he explains.

"I hate birds," I say.

For a while we continue our list, then Adrian puts his hand on my sweater arm. The brown fur congeals in his fingers. It is matted with sea-foam, and tiny perfect buds of marijuana.

"I hate everyone in Palos Verdes," he says. "Especially the girls."

First I'm happy about this, then I say, "What am I then?"

"You are a space alien, landed here. A wonderful girl from space—maybe from a faraway galaxy."

As we laugh, I remember what Jim said about the Adares—they're tacky gold diggers. Not talking, I watch Adrian's hands open and close. He's breathing very hard.

"I hate going home," he says.

"How could you hate living in that house?" I ask. "I thought that's what you guys wanted, the money."

"No. I wanted to stay in Manhattan Beach with my friends. I hate it here; you're the only cool person I've met." He looks at me and smokes.

I light a cigarette, pretending I know what to do with it. Then I turn away from him and put on the radio, staring into its flashing lights.

Finally I say, "Don't tell anyone I'm friends with you. I have to keep it secret."

"Here's a secret," he says, pulling my sweater to his lips, closing his mouth on it.

I smell fear and fur.

"Please close your eyes for a moment," he tells me. "I'll hate it if you peek."

I smile, and the craziness of it makes my skin flush red, but he does not stop at my sweater. As I close my eyes, I feel him touch my neck, then my cheek, and then he kisses me on the lips.

I can't look at him.

"I feel like the reverse of sick," I say, laughing.

"I hate sick girls."

"I hate kissing you," I say, smiling crazily at him.

"I knew I was going to kiss you. I knew it the minute I saw you today, Miss Fifteen."

I sit on the curb for a few minutes after he leaves, burning out on the pavement, so cool.

I'm holding my hand, staring at the black street. I look up at a white bird flying crookedly across the moon. Instantly exposed, like an X ray flash.

Then it is gone.

～～～

All night I dream about water. I slosh from one side of the bed to the other, riding waves while I sleep, aloft on the vanilla board, wearing a rubber wet suit that rubs my restless skin.

I'm half awakened when my mother creeps down the thick carpet of the hallway, tiptoeing over the places where the floorboards groan. Again I stir as she slowly renavigates the carpeting, chewing something fragrant with salt, and my dreams turn to a long spiral of water, wave after wave, visible in the shorelights blinking yellow and blue. My body is rocking, touched by cool water, held back by seaweed and a sudden warm current.

The bed is still rocking when the clock rings.

What I am feeling is this.

Desire.

～～～

I call Adrian's number the next night, but hang up suddenly. Jim's knocking on the door, a secret soft knock so my mother won't hear. He comes into my room, and settles down on the floor, feet up, the way he used to. He yawns and rolls his neck around casually, stretching.

I wait for him to ask for more money.

Instead he stalls, wiping the sweat from his forehead with a T-shirt from my folded laundry pile. He looks through our school yearbook, smiling at some of the pictures. After a while he puts it down and shifts onto his belly.

"I broke up with Heather," he says. "She was crying."

I go sit next to him on the floor; neither of us say anything for awhile. Then he tells me it's definitely *not* because our mother told him to. He says it's because he can never think of anything to say to Heather, her whole life revolves around her perfect family and her clothes. He tries to think of things to talk about in advance, but he can't remember them.

"She's so damn beautiful" is what he says over and over.

His head is back, his neck relaxed against the soft blue carpet.

Then he switches subjects. "Do you love surfing," he says, "I mean really, really *love* it?"

I say yes.

"I don't," he says. "I don't think I *love* it."

I tell him it's not true. Then I tell him how he looks on a wave, beautiful and free, hanging on to a powerful thrust, while it tries to throw him sideways. I talk to him as if I'm narrating a movie, I describe the deep gray-blue of the water, his gold blond hair, the way his hands push the water as he paddles. He interrupts me.

"I miss talking to Dad, sometimes," he says. "Even though I shouldn't."

I take his hand, but he pulls it away. He tells me maybe he wants to stay in my room until he dies.

∽∽∽

Later, I hear my mother breathing. She listens at the door for a few seconds before knocking. Then she barges in.

"Are you sick again, Jim?" she asks, kneeling in front of him.

"Sick?" he repeats, thinking. "Yes, I'm pretty sick of everything."

~~~

My father's on the morning news. He's going to do bypass surgery on Elizabeth Taylor. I see pictures of him wheeling a gurney around the cardiac ward, smiling, waving to his famous patients. I see a montage of film photographs of Elizabeth Taylor—then and now.

Ava must be happy, I decide. Elizabeth Taylor is a pretty lady, but she's much too old for my father.

When I call him at the hospital, he tells me that I'll need to take care of things while he's in Europe for a few months. He's taking Ava away; they're going to a conference so my father can tell European doctors how to fix hearts.

He explains how to avoid undertows in the water: *just swim sideways and then to the shore.* He warns me to pace myself when I run, so I won't get tired, and to study for three hours a day so I'll come out on top.

"Maybe it's not so bad underneath," I say, even though he doesn't know what I'm talking about.

Then I tell him what Jim said. That he misses him for real. My father tells me he's very happy to hear that.

"When I get back everything will be fine again, princess. You'll see."

I ask him if we can come live with him when he comes home. He clears his throat.

"We'll see."

⤝⤝⤝

At sunset the ocean comes alive. Wispy fronds of seaweed grab at the last rays of sunlight, sucking in stray nutrients. Electric eels swim against the tide looking for prey, while blackfish and sharks swish past silently. Ghost-white gulls are the last to emerge, floating in the moonlight, diving like arrows for fish among the waves.

I've convinced Jim to sneak out and go nightsurfing with me. While my mother watches TV, we pretend we're in our rooms doing homework. It's easy to sneak out my sliding glass door, gliding it quietly along its track, holding it with a soft towel so it won't bang shut.

Usually we laugh and clown around, but tonight Jim lies on his back, silent, looking at the stars jumbled in the sky. His mouth is moving, as if he is praying. He drifts farther and farther away from me.

He snickers, barely audible. "How can I protect anyone when I'm a joke?" His voice drops off, even lower. "A big, lame joke."

When I paddle closer he swerves away, warns me not to touch him.

"Maybe I shouldn't have hit Dad that time," he says. "He probably hates me now."

Then he says he's been trying to laugh with the guys, but everything he says sounds weird and wrong, as if someone else is talking through his mouth.

"They all want to come over to the house, they say it's strange that I never invite them."

He says he might stop talking soon, to everyone.

Then he takes off, free in the dark.

When we come home, Jim wades into the pool. He falls asleep in the chlorinated water, stomach down, hugging his surfboard. My mother hovers at the top of the stairs, calling for us to come out of the pool. She brings cookies on a tray, and even dangles her feet in the water once. When she finds a rolled-up joint floating in the water, she hides it quickly in a napkin.

Jim yawns, turning to his side. "I'm going to sleep here tonight, Mom, go inside, it's okay."

My mother watches, slumped against the deck.

I drag my own surfboard to the grass, and sleep with the fin between my legs.

〜〜〜

The next morning, while Jim's in the bathroom, she corners me in the kitchen.

"If you're giving him pot, I'll go to the police," she says. "I'll turn you in as a dealer."

"I'd never *give* him pot. He'd have to pay for it, if I were a dealer."

My mother switches tacks, like a wildly blowing sail, coming close, listing in anger.

"I heard your phone ring at two A.M. What kind of person would call you at an hour like that?"

"A supercool person. The kind of person who talks to me as if I'm not the number one freak of Palos Verdes—" I stop short of saying *"after you."*

Jim comes out of the bathroom, his face scrubbed red.

"Tell your sister to stop fighting me," my mother implores.

Jim runs back into the bathroom, slamming the door. I hear the sink running for a long time. He doesn't want us to know he's crying.

Later I hear noises in my mother's bedroom. I creep near the door to investigate.

Through the crack in the door I see a bag of nacho-flavored Doritos on her lap. Her mouth is orange. She is talking on the phone, weeping, to someone at a suicide prevention center.

"You don't taste anything after the first chips. You just fill up your mouth and swallow. I can eat three handfuls at a time. They aren't as filling as you'd think. But what would you know? You're just a young girl trained to listen to other people's problems. Don't you have enough problems of your own?"

My mother laughs into the receiver, munching. She sees my shadow under the door.

"Medina, dear," she calls out, "I seeeeee you, you little sneak. Always such a sneak, running around, spying on me. How would it feel if I got you back?"

I run out the door, heaving with speed, sprinting down the wooden steps that lead to the shore. My mother follows, standing on the top of the steps, screaming. All the surfers on the shore look upward.

She twirls around and around, the yellow bathrobe ballooning into the air. She is screaming at me, but her words are carried away by moving currents of air. Her legs are enormous, her underwear huge white expanses of material.

At first the surfers don't laugh, they only stare. There is a moment of silence until her voice floats down from the cliff.

"Did you people know Medina is a liar?" My mother jumps up and down, singing.

"Liar, liar, pants on fire, lalala a telephone wire."

When some of the Bayboys begin to laugh, I walk into the water with my head down, and keep swimming until I am tired.

The water roars, my legs and arms whip around in the eddies as I start to go under. I see the sky tilt, like a canopy bed coming down over my head, and I see clouds of white-caps hitting the breakwater. I see my mother still standing on the edge of the cliffs.

"Please fall off!" I yell.

But Jim comes out, ducking, pulling her quickly away.

The water is bursting and boiling, coming apart at its seams, but I am beginning to breathe again. Struggling, I swim toward the beach.

I retch a little when I climb out and hide from the surfers who watch.

Skeezer comes over, trying to help me up, but I fling his hand off my shoulder.

"It's okay, Medina," he says. "Don't cry."

I pretend the tears are seawater—I wipe them off with my hand.

"I'm fine," I say, running for the stairs. "I just wanted to go for a swim."

∽∽∽

The next day there's a pack of boys I hardly know from the north side of Palos Verdes. They're gathered, whispering, on the cliff. Weird Jack Wenger follows me. He has glinting braces and hairy legs. While I wait for Adrian, he circles and

circles like a shark, then moves in, asking me to go to Gull
Cove with him.

"I have a boyfriend now," I say.

He turns to his friends and laughs. "Medina Mason has a
boyfriend."

The other boys whisper, *"He's a Val."*

Jack comes toward me. "I heard all about your mother
taking her clothes off. I guess it runs in the family."

He knocks me to my knees, opening the Velcro fly of his
trunks, pulling my head close. "Do it, you crazy girl."

"Don't go too far, man," Jamie Weatherby says. "Jim
Mason's our friend. She's his sister."

Jack lets off, and I head-butt him hard in the groin. As
he goes down I run.

"Jesus, what took you so long?" I ask Adrian, when he finally pulls up on the curb. I climb into his car in my wet suit,
unzipping it while I climb in, shaking water all over the seat.

"You look good in black," he says.

All the guys are looking at us talking, shaking their heads
grimly.

"What's with those guys?" Adrian asks, adjusting his
sunglasses.

"I think one of them likes me."

"You're gonna get me killed." Adrian smiles, turning the
key in the ignition.

"What would you do if I kissed another guy?"

"Why?"

"Just asking."

I look at his hands opening and closing. "If you want to go
with another guy," he says, "then get out of my car right now."

I tell him, "I don't *really* want to. I just wanted to see what
you would say."

"Don't play games like a little fifteen-year-old."

I pick up a cigarette, trying not to smile, but I can't help it.

～～～

I smile all through dinner as my brother gets angrier. He's been inside all day, cleaning the house, too embarrassed to come out and face the guys.

Neither of us talks to my mother. She stomps off into her room.

"You have to stay in and help me take care of Mom now," he says. "We've got to stick together."

I tell him I couldn't stand to be locked up all day with her, and he shouldn't either. I tell him he isn't her husband, even though she treats him like he is.

His eyes narrow. "You'd just rather be with that Val," he says, suddenly merciless, pinning my head against the wall. "You don't care about anyone but him."

I look at him and say, "At least I go out. I don't clean toilets for Mama."

When he punches, I fight back. My mother comes from her room, separating us with her hand. She slaps me in the face, hard, and says, "Get out of my house, girl."

～～～

Adrian's fumbling around in the ashtray for a joint, lighting it, putting it in my mouth, then in his. I ask him why he likes me, because I'm not even pretty.

"You're not pretty," he says, drawing on the joint, "but you're beautiful."

Later when we're stoned, he tells me again how beautiful I am, how he can't stop looking at me. I shrink back in the velour seats and laugh.

"I'm like a man, and men aren't beautiful."

"You are, man," he answers. "You're like the most beautiful man I've ever known."

At midnight, he tries to start the car. I grab the keys and throw them out the window, admitting the truth.

"I'm sure my mother locked the doors. If I go home I'll have to sleep in the yard in a sleeping bag," I say, flushing, not looking at him.

He holds me close, tells me it's okay, we can sleep in the Mustang tonight.

"I've never slept in a boy's car before."

I recline on the seat, stretching toward him.

"Also, I've never had sex before," I say, looking down. "At least not really."

He sits very straight, stiff like a wax statue, all of a sudden flushing red.

"You're not a virgin, Medina. You don't have to pretend."

"It doesn't count if you don't like the person," I say.

All he says is, "Goodnight."

Twenty minutes later I'm almost asleep, warm under Adrian's coat, lulled by the soft sway of the waves. I feel his hand on my neck and lean toward him, stretching my body over the seats. His hand moves across my face, pushing the jacket aside, touching my shoulder. I bite his finger softly and then suck on it until he moans.

"Do you like me more than the rest of the girls?"

"Yes," he says. "I like you more than Tina, Joan, Mary, Darcy, and Constance." Then he laughs, low and teasing.

It isn't easy to lie back in a car, even in the comfortable velour backseat of the Mustang. We slip our hands into each other's clothes, sweaty, breathing hard, fogging the windows with heat. I move against his hand, swaying to the sound of the water for twenty liquid minutes, faster and faster, until it happens.

"That was so cool," he says. "You should have seen your face."

I laugh, and tell him I *have* seen my face. "I've looked in a mirror while I'm doing it to myself."

He stares at me, raising an eyebrow, then lets his breath out slowly. "There's no one like you," he says, pulling me roughly on top of him.

We wake at dawn, to the sound of firetrucks whirring and zooming past. We peek out sleepily and then fall back in the seats. A policeman taps on the window at six thirty.

"All right, Miss Mason, move along now," he says, surveying the car with his flashlight.

Adrian starts the car, cute, blinking like a frog in the raw morning light.

My brother is waiting in my room, eyes red and swollen. I crouch low in case he punches. Instead he smiles at me. "I've been up all night. I thought you ran away for good with that Val."

"I'm sorry about last night, Jim," I say, wrapping him in a blanket. "I shouldn't have said that about the toilets."

He waves his hand as if clearing the air between us and tells me to forget about it. He tries to snap me with the blanket, and misses.

"So are you gonna come surfing with me, or are you gonna lie around all morning like a troll?" he says, connecting.

Jim and I are surfing close to the rocks when he falls, hitting his head on the reef. I jump off my board and swim to him fast. The salt water is red with his blood.

"How come I always fall now?" he says, face very white, flicking blood from his hand into the waves.

"Everyone wipes out, Jim. It's no big deal."

He swishes the water, watching drops of blood mingle with the tide and slowly float away.

"You never wipe out," he says. "You're better than me now."

He giggles strangely, says maybe he's more like our mother, a freak.

I'm careful not to insult her, not wanting another fight. "I thought I was the freak. Isn't that what everybody says?"

When he doesn't answer, or even look at me, I splash him gently. He watches the dots of silver water arc upward, flinching when they hit him in the face. Then he shakes his head, as if waking up from a heavy sleep.

"I'll tell you a secret." His eyes suddenly focus on me, deep green, violent. "You're the strong one, Medina." He laughs again, a deep belly laugh, as if he'd just told a funny joke.

Then he tells me everyone knows it, especially our mother.

As we take the next wave to the beach he rides close to me, rubbing his face with salt water to clean it.

The rest of the day at the beach he is mellow, cool to me. I sit right by his side and talk to him. He takes three black pills, swallows them, deliberately looking at me. Then he tells me again how sorry he is about last night.

"I get so mad. Sometimes I wish everyone would just die."

I look at him, scared. He continues talking.

"And being around all these perfect P.V. people makes it

worse." He gestures to the pretty girls sitting in a ring on the beach.

"Forget them, we're our own tribe, just me and you. They don't understand anything about us."

My brother relaxes a bit, even smiles. "I think about that a lot—about sticking with your tribe until you die." He puts his head against my shoulder, yawning. His eyes are peaceful. Then he closes them.

When he wakes up, we have a long sandfight, and then we go surfing again. In the water I ask him about the pills.

"They're trippy," he says evasively. "They make you feel really good."

"Can I have one then?"

He tells me no, they're only good if you need them. "You don't need them, Medina, you never fall."

I want to ask him more details, but I'm afraid it will spoil the good mood between us. Instead I tease him, pointing to a blond girl in a white bikini.

"Are you sure you wouldn't rather hang out with a nice girl like her?"

"I'm tired of plastic girls," Jim says, looking at Cindy Spink as she walks past. "You don't know how tired."

❦❦❦

The next day Jim and I practice swimming from one end of the pool to the other without taking a breath. He dives deep under the water when our mother calls to him through the window.

"Pretend you don't hear her," he whispers, motioning me out of the pool.

We go to my room and I blast the music really loud, getting ready for a surf session. We dance around to punk rock, getting amped before running out my sliding glass door, racing each other to the cliff stairs. But when we get there, I see Adrian's car parked at the cliffs. I smile nervously and wave to him. Jim shakes his head.

"It's never gonna be like it used to, is it?" Then he walks off. When I run after him, he tells me to go away, surf with my new boyfriend, see if he cares. But it's easy to see he's glad that I won't.

At Pratt Point, he doesn't go in the water. He throws rocks at it instead.

～〜～〜

The waves are unbelievable today, another storm from Mexico. I run to my brother's room, excited. A heavy camping-sleeping bag is tied over the curtain rods, held in place with duct tape. It is so dark that at first I don't see him. Then I hear him rustle in the bed, a lump under the army blankets on the far side.

"I'm not hungry, Mom."

"It's me, stupid," I say. "Get up. The bay's huge, you've got to get up."

"Go away," he whispers. "I can't get up. I feel terrible."

"I'm not lying," I say. "It's seven feet!"

He rubs his head as if he has a terrible fever, his eyes are closed, and he is rocking. "Do you have any pot?" he asks.

My mother comes in from the hall. "Don't ever give him any pot, Medina."

My brother groans. "Would the two of you shut the fuck up!"

"Jim," my mother says, "don't you dare talk to me like

that." Then she turns to me. "Don't talk to your brother about the waves."

These are the biggest waves I've ever seen. A few guys are paddling out in the water, crowds of girls watch from the shore. Skeezer, sitting on dry land, looks at my board, laughs, and says I'm crazy. Ted slaps me on the back and says, "Go!" Everyone is watching me as I look at the huge walls of water. I head for the rocks, trying to smile.

Storm oceans are thicker, heavier, weighted with churning sand. The waves, deep ocean swells, are arctic cold in some spots, suddenly warm in others.

Waiting for a lull, I start to paddle out, aiming for the horizon. Seaweed thrashes around my ankles. The sun is half-hidden, orange, dull.

The set starts before I'm ready. The water level suddenly changes, rising upward, growing taller, wider, impossibly vast. The ocean surges backward as if sucking in its breath, pulling everything toward its core. Trying to avoid being sucked in too soon, I aim the nose of my board to the right, only half in control. As I paddle frantically, a guy drops in too early, falling through the air, screaming into the wind. The wave pulls itself up like a mountain being born; it crests, then begins to fold, hissing. Broiling spray hits my face from six yards away.

At the break line, the guys are lined up, tense and focused. A few smile, watching me struggle toward them. Most don't even notice. As I approach, heart beating fast, Charlie Becker motions for me to line up next to him. "I see you've improved your paddling skills," he calls out, winking at me. Then he tells me I can take his turn, but I better get ready, it's coming up fast.

The view from the backside of a wave is surreal. Surfers drop off the edge of the world, free-falling into space. As I watch them go, Charlie tells me not to be scared. "I'm not *too* scared," I say, shivering.

"Good," he says gravely, eyes twinkling. "Because this one's for you." He gives my board a shove, calls to the guys that this is my wave.

"Nooooooooo," I scream, dropping in, suddenly weightless, headed for the bottom, nose first. The wave begins to fold in on itself as I careen to the side, ducking down, wind whistling in my ears. Then I'm inside a long, blue cavern. It's eerily soundless except for the noise of my board cutting through a thick wall of rushing liquid. The wave gets softer as it unfolds, looser, slower, more forgiving. I relax, letting the shape of the wave guide me across the bay. Just before it ends, I look at the people on the shore. Even though I know Skeezer's watching, I can't help it. I do a little dance, shaking my butt, moving my arms up and down like a disco queen.

When I paddle out again, my teeth are chattering, arms numb, face frozen. An older guy nicknamed Teacher, because he wears glasses, paddles up beside me.

"Excellent," he says, slapping my back so hard it knocks the wind out of me.

⌒⌒⌒

Later, I burst through the door. Jim is on the couch, eating Count Chocula frosted cereal from the box with his hands. He is shaking, like he's cold, and looking at the cartoons on the television.

"Come on, Medina, narrate," he says.

Instead I tell him about the huge waves, how everyone saw, how I only fell twice.

"It was so rad," I say, "like taking off on a 747 plane."

"Please shut up and narrate," he says, face tense, eyes closed.

When I do the cartoon sound effects, Jim starts to laugh.

"Bugs is waiting under a bush, he clobbers Elmer with a pail. Elmer's head turns into a pail, it pops back into shape . . ."

"I love that," he says, standing up. "I always feel better when you do that."

"That's all folks," I say, imitating Elmer Fudd, trying to smile.

He laughs and leaves the house, slamming the door behind him.

"Let him go," I tell my mother as she follows. "Please."

All night I hear the storm waves crash against the side of the cliff below the house, bigger and bigger. Jim comes in at midnight, walking unsteadily down the hall, trying to tiptoe over the loud spots on the floor. My mother stays in her room eating chips from a bag. I hear the pop and the pug dog wiggling. The waves rise ever higher, crashing without mercy against the rocks, until no one can sleep. We all meet in the kitchen at two.

"Don't talk about the waves," my mother says to me. "Don't say anything."

Jim stares at me intensely, laughing, his pupils alert black dots. His skin is waxy and moist, his hands trembling.

Excitedly he says, "I heard you kicked ass out there today, girl. I heard even Skeezer wouldn't go out. Congratufuckinglations."

"Don't say a word," my mother says, standing up quickly, slamming the refrigerator door shut. A jar of mayonnaise shatters on the floor.

"Did you almost die?" Jim says.

I smile at him; I don't say a word.

"I'm going out surfing with you tomorrow," he says. "I feel *so* good."

·

Tide

❧❧❧

·

At dawn the storm is over. Everything slows to a dead stop.

The water under my house shimmers like blood and glitter.

A few Bayboys laze on the cliffs, sitting dumbly on their boards, smoking burning joints and bickering. Seagulls cruise overhead, confused, not knowing where to land. A local news crew arrives.

"Red tide is a natural occurrence, a surge of tiny one-celled sea organisms called phytoplankton, which can un-expectedly proliferate and spread over a large area . . ."

The television broadcast goes on all morning, as reporters try to explain to the bewildered citizens what has overtaken their shores. The red glow in the water is due to an invasive microscopic plant, probably washed in by the storm. Each liter of sea water contains millions.

The tide itself is not harmful to humans, but it is deadly to fish, eating up oxygen in the water, so fish literally drown.

"The only possible danger to human health comes from rotting fish," a newscaster warns. "Citizens should avoid all areas near the water."

∽∽∽

They shut down the tennis club on the second day.

Closed until further notice, by order of the U.S. Health Department due to the red tide. We will in-

form members by telephone of all changes in status.
Sincere apologies,
The management.

~~~~~~

Everyone has his own view of the red tide. Especially people with an ocean view.

"They aren't telling us everything," Marge Paxton says to Marlene Smalley on the cliff. "I mean they can't just shut down the tennis club, unless it's an emergency! We shouldn't be breathing this air. It's scary."

"How can something safe smell so bad?" Buffy Peters asks. Then she squeals. "Look, your footprints are glowing!"

Buffy's husband peers at the tide with a flashlight, holding his nose, grimacing.

Terri Miller asks her best friend, Sally Jones, "What do I do with the kids? They're stuck in the rec room. Maybe we should wear gas masks?"

Skeezer sneaks up on me. "Let's push Medina in," he yells.

~~~~~~

The third day of the tide, octopus tentacles begin to wash up against the rocks, silvery-red, leaving phosphorescent trails in the tide pools. Porpoises lay on the sand, inert, like soggy leather sacks. A whale maroons herself against the pylons of the jetty, swaying gently in the fog until she dies.

The stink seeps through living rooms and gardens, into ocean-view master bedrooms. And there it stays, over the women who recline on their beds, scented towels over their eyes, fingers dangling in bowls of ice water. It hangs over the doctors and lawyers, who drink an extra belt of Scotch and curse.

"Damn that damn stuff," an angry man screams into the night, "damn it to hell, already."

Towel girls play video games and watch television under sun lamps. They call each other's private phone lines and laugh about their parents' hushed arguments. The surfers hide in their rec rooms, locking the doors, smoking weed. The mothers call each other nervously and direct their maids to spray Lysol all over the rugs and couches twice every hour.

Families are at home together for the first time in years. They aren't sure what to say to one another. They try to make the best of it.

A few families—the Scudders, the Arnolds—move to their second homes in Mammoth Mountain or Hawaii. They leave maids behind with instructions to burn potpourri night and day to lift the smell from the Persian carpets.

Teams of scientists come in U.S. Fish and Game Department vans to study the tide, armed with sonar webs and telescopic cameras. They put up signs along the worst of the beaches.

DANGER. DO NOT SWIM. DO NOT FISH. UNSAFE WATER.

People gather in knots to discuss the tide. They call a town meeting, the first town meeting in seventeen years. Fish and Game Department scientists tell the citizens gathered in the school gymnasium that this is the worst case of red tide they have ever seen.

"Tides like this are *not usually dangerous*," they emphasize. "However, this one is so thick, those close to the shore should take *unusual precautions*."

Listening to theories, the citizens grow angry and restless. They whisper together, attacking the common enemy, misery, stink.

At eight thirty, Ada Pernell finally stands up and asks what everyone really wants to know.

"When will that smell go away? When are you going to do something about it?"

"Yes, hear, hear!" someone else exclaims, as if in a Lion's Club meeting.

The room hums angrily like a hive. As people grumble that it is their taxes that pay for things like the Fish and Game Department, a fire engine roars past, its lights flashing red against the neutral scientific charts and graphs.

"Forget your explanations," someone shouts over the siren. "We want results."

The fathers can't will away the red tide or have it fired. The mothers can't redecorate it or ignore its presence. The kids can't surf in it, or smoke near it, or have sex in its bays.

And each day the tide quietly spreads.

∽∽∽

Summer school is mandatory for students in the Mentally Gifted Minors program so that we can complete early college courses. It's also mandatory for any student who carries a C average or worse. The quads are full of underachievers in the summer; angry, bored, rich bitches looking for a fight, flicking cheese balls at my legs while I study on the grass.

In the second week of the tide, sudden offshore winds bring the smell to our campus, sickening students and teachers in the airless classrooms. Summer school is shut down in the third week.

⮎⮎⮎

I won't need to fight them this summer. There will be no taunts about my mother—*"whale, pig, boat, hog"*—in the hallways. It's the first year I won't hit anyone with hairbrushes or fists, or bite someone's arm to the point of blood. I will not kick Sydelle Braverman's thin shin, or spit in Marcy Knight's Clinique-perfect face. As I dump the contents of my locker into the trash can, I smile and give myself a high five.

But later at home, my stomach hurts as I wrap my surfboard in clean towels for storage. I wind them carefully like a triage bandage, around and around its beautiful vanilla skin.

⮎⮎⮎

The tide hasn't reached the shores of Manhattan Beach, a city twenty miles away. Adrian says we should go there.

"We could surf the pier," he says. "I dare you to come."

But he knows why I'm not supposed to go. By unspoken agreement, no one from Palos Verdes is supposed to surf outside beaches, because then we'd have to reciprocate and let outsiders come here.

Adrian pushes. "I thought you weren't like them."

"True," I say, undecided.

⮎⮎⮎

Jim's been sleeping all afternoon. I spy on him, trying to make loud coughing noises so he'll wake up and listen to my idea, but he's huddled under the covers, not moving.

I get three empty banana crates from Lunada Bay Market and line them up side to side in the garage. Then I take the handlebars off my old bicycle and attach rubber bungee cords to the bars. Next I get a screw gun and mount the handlebars into the wood, tightening as much as I can. Finally I take a piece of old carpet from the dog's bed and put it over the crates.

"Voilà," I say to Jim, dragging him to the garage. "Here's our new paddling machine."

I turn on the radio and lie down on the crates, pulling at the pieces of rubber as hard as I can, feeling my tricep muscles constrict.

"I'm going to be way stronger than old Skeez when the tide's gone," I say.

My brother is laughing while he watches me tug on the bungees, and he says the paddle machine is super cool. I tell him we could pretend I'm surfing for real if he'd narrate a good set for me.

At first he doesn't know what to say. He thinks for a long time, his eyebrows wrinkled, his eyes tightly closed. Then he starts to speak softly.

"Okay, there's a big set coming in—"

I interrupt, excited. "What color is the water? How fast is it coming?"

"Shhhhh," he says. "It's gray-green with whitecaps, it's a south swell, there's no one out but us. Skeezer's watching from the cliffs, all the guys are—"

I interrupt again, impatient. "How far away is the wave?"

"Twenty yards away, it's loud like thunder, coming really fast. You better start paddling."

He goes on, getting excited now, telling me I've got to paddle like I've never paddled before. "Hurry, faster, you're gonna miss it."

I pull on the rubber as hard as I can, imagining the wave setting up. I kick with my legs, furious, grabbing on to the side of the crate like it's a rail, feeling the swoosh and motion, hearing rocks tumble in the surf.

I push up with my arms, letting go of the bungees, rising on my feet, awash in the moment. I flail around with my arms, swatting at the hot garage air, hanging ten on the crate until it topples.

"I could see the wave," Jim says, eyes shining. "I could really see it."

At midnight I'm on the phone, telling Adrian about the paddle machine. He says he wishes he could see it, but we should go to Manhattan Beach where we can ride real swells.

I tell him if we go we have to take my brother.

"He'll like you, once he meets you," I say uncertainly. "I'm sure of it."

∽∽∽

A moth bats softly against the kitchen window, trapped. My mother crushes it with a newspaper.

"I hate those things," she says, sighing.

Jim glowers at his breakfast as I try to chew sausage in the rotten air. I'm telling him about the clean water in Manhattan Beach, how the three of us can sneak away and surf there.

"I thought it was going to be you and me now," he says.

He gets angrier by the second, looking out at the water, muttering and holding his nose. When I spear a last piece of egg, Jim knocks the fork out of my hand.

"Just because your Val boyfriend has a car doesn't mean it's okay to betray everybody."

"You can come, too," I say, flushing. "There isn't a *real* law against going to other beaches."

"Trolls, dickheads, fags, idiots. That's who's at other beaches," Jim says.

"If your brother doesn't want to go," my mother says quietly, "I'm sure he has good reason."

Jim cackles, a disturbing sound that causes my mother to look up from her plate and say, "Jim, come on, don't, please?"

As she chews a rasher of meat, we all swallow, looking at each other. Jim stabs the table with the tines of his fork, telling me I'm a traitor.

"Please don't go with that guy," he says, blinking.

My mother eats and chews angrily, looking at us, back and forth like a tennis match. My brother pops his knuckles, his throat moving, a puff of hostile *sssss* sounds coming out. I waver at the door, torn.

My mother smiles at Jim, holding out her hands to be touched, baiting like a sport fisherman, reeling, catching. Telling him how much she appreciates his loyalty to his friends.

"And to me," she adds quickly.

As a reward, she opens her purse and hands him forty dollars.

He gathers up the money in his hands and then lies down on the floor, shaking with sobs, a strange froggy croak erupting from his throat. My mother moves close, getting down on the carpet with him.

A single cloud covers the sun, coming from nowhere. We both move even closer to him. I speak first.

"Okay, I'll stay with you. We can rent movies, maybe *Jaws* . . ."

I smile at him, whispering the *Jaws* music: da nuh, da nuh, da nuh.

I try to laugh, but it's too dry. I need water.

∽∽∽

It's hot and crowded at Marineland. The air smells like fish and burnt cotton candy sugar.

I'm with Adrian waiting for the dolphin show to start because Adrian's writing a paper on dolphins for his science class. We're here to study how they live in captivity.

Sunburnt kids are throwing greasy popcorn into the murky water, hoping to lure fish to the top of the tank. Instead, shrieking, overfed seagulls swoop low, fighting over the morsels, mauling each other with their sharp orange beaks.

People clap when the trainer comes out from behind a white wall, wearing a tuxedo wet suit. A chute opens and the first dolphin swims out. He's wearing a plastic chef's hat, Velcroed around his head with a white plastic strap. The dolphin circles the small tank quickly before picking a piece of fish out of the trainer's hand.

"Ladies and gentlemen, it's Bobo, the gourmet dolphin!"

The trainer explains that dolphins aren't usually finicky eaters, but Bobo is an exception. He's used to hand-fed mackerel meal, enriched with vitamins.

Everyone laughs except Adrian, who writes something down on a pad of paper, shaking his head. Next, three more dolphins swim out, jumping over high ropes and getting pieces of smelly tuna as a reward. Then loud, jazzy music comes on, and the trainer reappears riding two dolphins around the tank like skis, waving to the crowd.

That's when Adrian stands up to leave.

On the way out, we have to stop at the souvenir stand to get our parking stub validated. There's a huge inflatable killer whale hanging from the ceiling; blown glass dolphins and fuzzy sea lions are neatly lined up on the shelves.

"Do you want me to buy you something?" Adrian asks. "Isn't that what boyfriends are supposed to do?"

"Are you my boyfriend?" I ask, freezing in place, not looking at him.

"Of course." He smiles. "If it's okay with you."

I squeeze his fingers. "I already told everyone you were."

We drive to Menlo Park, high above the bluffs where you can barely smell the red tide. I'm eating Kraft Parmesan Cheese out of the green metallic can, spilling a few grains into my palm, then licking them off. Adrian's writing something on his pad of paper, but he looks up when I shake the can again.

"Do you think this is gross?" I ask, wiping my hand on the grass before I pour more cheese into it. Adrian thinks for a moment, and says it's not half as gross as a dolphin wearing a hat. Then he writes again.

"Jim loves dolphins," I say carefully, telling Adrian about my brother's book on dolphins and whales.

Adrian puts down his pad of paper. He lifts an eyebrow and shifts position. "He doesn't seem like the type who would care about animals."

I tell Adrian that Jim isn't easy to explain.

"You two aren't anything alike," Adrian persists. "I don't see how you could be so close."

I tell Adrian he's wrong. Then I tell him he wouldn't understand about twins since he's an only child. I explain that Jim and I are closer than anyone else, and we always will be.

Instead of getting mad, Adrian lies down in the grass,

massaging his temples as if he has a headache. Then he tells me he used to wish he had a sister, but Ava never wanted any more kids. I remind him about what'll happen if Ava marries my father.

We look at each other, scared. Then he wags his eyebrows, rubbing his hands together, perverted.

"Incest *is* best," he says, pulling me into his lap, tickling me.

Then we're laughing so hard I almost pee.

"I told you your father wants to forget all about us," my mother says later, when he misses his scheduled call that night. "Maybe he'll just stay in France."

"He's flying back in August," I say, looking at Jim, prodding him.

"I'll bet he travels first class," my mother says.

After dinner, I watch Jim staring into space, flying his hand in the air like an airplane. Our dog Puggles is in his lap, snoring. I see the phone off the hook, knocked under the cushions.

"Look! Puggles knocked over the phone again. I bet Dad did try to call, but he couldn't get through."

Jim crashes his hand into the carpet.

"It doesn't matter anyway. The divorce is final in two weeks. He probably won't want to talk to me anymore because he's got a new son now."

South-facing homes like ours are the worst hit. As the tide thickens, more and more neighbors begin to evacuate their dream homes. They pack luggage with the essentials— tennis gear and sun oil—then head off to points south, Mazatlàn or Cabo.

They go in groups, the Weatherbys with the Cuttings and Snells. The Jewish families go together. A few families go to their second homes in Newport Beach.

The kids go reluctantly.

"Mom, I don't want to go to Mexico. It's so boring there, and you and Dad always get sunburned and complain about the food. Besides there's no surf in Cabo. Nothing for us to do."

But anything is better than the stench of rotting fish and the closing of the tennis club. The families arrange to meet each other for drinks at a new resort, to have a tennis game and a glass or two of chardonnay.

"The Playa has a good wine list. The best in Mexico—we'll meet there. We'll make do, even have some fun. We'll survive—Olé!"

∽∽∽

"We're alone on Via Neve, practically," I report a few days later. "Even the Grahams are gone."

"Well I'm glad they're gone, let them find someone else to gossip about," my mother says, turning to Jim. She puts her arm around him, squeezing tight. He stands stiff, not looking at her.

"That family at Donner Pass ate each other when they were trapped."

"Jim," my mother says, "don't joke like that. Make us a sandwich. There's turkey and mayo."

•

Fire

〜〜〜

•

A brush fire starts at ten o'clock in the tall, dry grass of Gull Hill. Fire engine sirens echo from the rocks, red and blue lights reflect off the water, people and peacocks scream in the dark.

The barren hillside is gone in twenty minutes, orange licks of flame jumping from tree to tree like monkey tails. Even in the fog, columns of smoke are visible, rising, funneling darkly away.

Jim is alone on the curb in front of the house when I run down the driveway. He is smiling for the first time in days.

"Look at it go!"

"I'm scared; what if it comes here?" I say.

He puts my head on his shoulder, brushing the ash and smoke from my hair, reassuring me.

"Fire and water don't mix, stupid."

A breeze comes up, and we hold our noses, nauseated by the smell of red tide.

"It's so beautiful," he says, choking. "Doesn't it look like a wave?"

꿈꿈꿈

At midnight I lie on the bed with a wet towel over my face, trying to keep the smells out. Small dark shapes dart by, disappearing under the rocks on the cliffside. When the phone rings, I jump to grab it before my mother does.

"Wow," Adrian says. "Are you okay?"

"Cats are running around like crazy."

"It's arson," Adrian says. "They found matches and stuff in the glen. The cops are swarming the place. Marge Paxton is on TV."

When I run to the living room looking for Jim, I see Marge Paxton on TV, being interviewed by a pretty newscaster. The camera is zooming in on the fires and then on her face.

The newscaster says, "I'm here live, in the exclusive, gated community of Palos Verdes, with Marge Paxton, home owner."

Marge bursts in. "First that tide, then this fire; what's next? The locusts?" She sweeps her pageboy to the side, looks angrily into the camera, and speaks. "Whoever did this, I hope you're happy."

Jim laughs when she says this.

"No you don't," he says. "You hope they'll die."

∽∽∽

My mother doesn't care about the fires or the tide.

Money. That's what she's talking about tonight. Piles of money stretching out to the water, oceans of bills that will float to Dr. Phil Mason.

All day we've been watching local news interviews with wealthy Palos Verdes families. My mother is indignant about the beautiful interior of Mrs. Paxton's house. She lists the prices of the Paxtons' antiques and rugs as the camera pans through their living room.

"It looks just like your father's house," she says. "He spent plenty on that fancy designer from England. He never let *me* buy nice things for *this* house."

She says she's tired of being poor, Jim deserves better. She hums softly.

"Don't worry, sweetheart, I have a good plan," she tells Jim, "and your father isn't here to stop me."

"Red Rover, Red Rover—send the catalogues right over. And row, row, row your boat upstream, Phil, because merrily, merrily we're going to buy a few things we need."

"Shhhh," Jim says, watching a citizen's fire-watch posse gather angrily in front of the bay. "Look. Even Mr. Chaplain is scared."

"Maybe the arsonist will do us a favor and get your father's house next time." My mother stretches, sprays a little cheese from a can onto her potato chips.

"Then he'd be poor, and we'd have to move for sure," I say, glaring at her.

"He'd get the insurance. Your father is very shrewd."

"He's still the one paying for this house," I insist, looking at Jim.

"Oh yes. He'll pay," my mother promises.

When dinner is over, my mother tries to command my brother's attention.

"Look, Jim, we can buy nice things like everybody else's now."

She spreads the cards out, picking one with her eyes closed. With American Express Platinum, she orders Godiva chocolates. With Mastercard she arranges on the telephone for the family portrait to be repainted. As her orders are accepted, she becomes more sure of herself, arrogant even, hurrying along the operator.

"UPS it, Fed Ex it, next-day delivery. Send those things right over." She laughs into the receiver. "Run, run, run as fast as you can."

Mrs. Phil Mason the cards say. They say it in writing.

❧❧❧

A family of hawks circles the black trees on the hill, diving near to the ground, looking for animals displaced by the fire. A few surfers, towel girls, and remaining mothers are there too, looking. Yellow police barriers crisscross the edge of the hill, people line up just behind them.

❧❧❧

Cami Miller and her friends are staring at us in the Mustang parked on the edge of Sueno Street. I smile at Cami, then bark at her.

"Why'd you do that?" Adrian says, laughing.

"Please, swear you won't laugh," I say, chewing on my nails.

Then I tell Adrian what they spray-painted on my locker in red acrylic: *Bitch. Slut. Whore. Bitch. Hate You.*

Then I tell him how they wait, every year, near the MGM halls after school with water balloons, and how I eat lunch alone in back of the science quad, hidden behind a jacaranda tree. For a minute I wait silently, with my eyes down. Adrian doesn't laugh.

❧❧❧

At noon the next day, we're parked at Manhattan Beach Pier.

The public beach sign in the parking lot has been sprayed over so it reads NOT A PUBLIC BEACH. A bus bench is graffitied: LOCALS ONLY. GET OUT YOU SUCK SUCKERS.

I'm afraid of surfing here, but Adrian grabs the vanilla

board off the rack on top of the Mustang, opening the door.

"Look. I won't even tell them where you're from. I promise."

The group of surfers all eye me curiously and say hello to Adrian, slapping him on the back, giving him a warm, friendly beer.

"I've known these guys for years," he whispers, "since my mother was married to husband number two."

"Ade got himself a rich chick," Derrick Wong says right off. Another guy says, "Do you have a sister?"

"We're not rich," I say, laughing.

"Come off it," Derrick insists, kissing my hand. "You even have teeth like a rich girl."

After a few more questions, I have to admit I'm from Lunada Bay.

"Lunada?" Derrick asks. "Whoa. I wanna go! Tell the Bayboys I'm your houseboy or your maid's poor little son from China."

"She doesn't have a maid," Adrian says, tightly holding my hand.

"He does," I say, pinching him.

Then we all smoke a little weed, talk about what's been going on in Manhattan Beach since Adrian left. I listen, smoking, until I can relax.

"Okay, surfer girl, show these guys how great you are," Adrian says.

"Go with me," I beg.

"Come on, shredder. You go and I'll watch."

While I put on my wet suit, I listen from the sand, spying. Adrian sits in the middle of a secret surfer's circle, smiling as they try to pry information out of him.

"You just came back to see how the other half surfs," they joke with him, "the better half."

"Cradle robbery, man, is that what you rich guys do?"

"She's skinny, and living the lux life for sure, but she seems cool. I'd say you're a lucky man, Ade."

"I didn't know those girls talked to us lowdowns. You're still a lowdown, no matter what place you move to. What did they do? Open the gates of Palos Verdes and let you all come down slumming?"

"Look," Adrian tells them. "If my mother didn't fuck some doctor, I'd still be here, and you know it."

"What's it like up in those hills, brother?" asks Derrick Wong, diffusing the tension. "I hear you get arrested up there for driving a Pinto. I hear you've got to have a Beemer or something."

Derrick slaps Adrian on the back, and does a perfect imitation of a P.V. boy. He gets the smug, lazy voice just right.

"Why don't you just get into your twenty-five-dollar car, and drive back to the Valley, where you can serve me a burger with a smile on your ugly face. And you can say thank you . . . massa."

When I paddle out for a wave, they stop talking.

Strange conch-shaped waves come fast and hard, then break very close to the shore. Compared to the long, smooth tubes of Palos Verdes, the waves at Manhattan Beach Pier are harsh like the first jolt of an earthquake. Two seconds after I take off, I realize I'm out of control; the water lifts me high, bucks underneath, and then ends without warning.

I wipe out badly and swim, ashamed, looking for my board. Derrick's deep voice calls out, "Get a leash," but I ignore him.

From the safety of the whitewash, I study the patterns in the current; the height between the crest and trough, the time it takes for the swash to break. After watching for a few sets, I paddle out again.

This time, instead of resisting the violent swerves and thrusts, I let my body relax until I feel fluid and flexible. Finally I stand, riding a wave without falling. There's sand in my teeth and bruises blooming on the balls of my feet. My heart is beating extra fast, my mouth is numb with cold and salt.

I feel beautiful.

⌒⌒⌒

The boys high-five me later on the shore, crowding around, winking at Adrian. "I've never seen a chick surf like that!"

"I told you," he says, shrugging.

"And, it's good to know someone from Lunada Bay." Derrick smiles. *"Real* good."

I smile back, but an invisible wall divides us.

⌒⌒⌒

A thick chain is stretched from one end of Palos Verdes Drive to the next, stopping all cars from entering. Police have set up a roadblock. They stand in a line, peering into the cars with flashlights and badges. They motion Mexicans, dented cars, anyone they don't recognize as a citizen of Palos Verdes to the side of the road for further inspection.

"She's okay," one policeman says to another, waving us past with a baton. "That's Phil Mason's daughter."

But before we drive off, he gives us a little advice.

"Don't park anywhere tonight, Miss Mason; go straight home where it's safe. There's a dangerous criminal on the loose."

"Ooooh! Maybe the arsonist is watching," I tease as we drive away. "Maybe you should take me home where it's safe."

Opening and closing his hands, Adrian admits he has to go home soon to study for a calculus test. I tell him it's too early to go home, plus I want to try the strawberry daiquiris that are sitting in the cooler.

"Sorry, but I have to study, Medina. U.C. Davis won't let me in unless I pass these last summer school classes."

When I ask how much longer until he leaves, he stares straight ahead. "A few months."

I tell him it's not fair that he gets to go, but I have to wait.

"Wouldn't it be funny if I ran away?" I say, closing my eyes. "I could come with you . . ."

"Right," Adrian says. "We'd be laughing all the way to jail."

We drive around not talking, looking for a spot away from the red tide. We park far away from the cliffs, under the eaves of the Wayfarer's Chapel.

"We have twenty minutes," Adrian says, setting the timer on his watch.

I drink five electric-colored daiquiris in a can, quickly. The sky starts to spin. Still I drink.

"You're getting wasted," Adrian says, sitting up.

"You're getting away," I tell him, sinking.

I pass out after Adrian drops me off, burrowing under my woolly frog blanket, but soon I'm awakened by smoke and sirens. The Portuguese Bend fire starts at eleven, coyotes howl in the hills and fire trucks wail, hopscotching up the thin, dry trails.

My head is on fire from the daiquiris. I run to the bathroom, nauseated, breathing in smoke and red tide. After half an hour, I creep out the door, holding my stomach, shaking, white.

"Oh, God," my mother says, standing in front of the door. "Are you pregnant? I knew this would happen."

I try to stand straight. "No, I'm on the pill."

"How did you get that?" she asks, and then she says, "I don't want to know, that's your business, not mine."

❧❧❧

"So, were they trolls?" Jim asks the next day, trying to be casual.

"No, they were supercool," I tell him bluntly, tensed for a fight. But Jim only picks at his nails and jokes sarcastically.

"It's been pretty cool here, too. First we played cards, then Monopoly. Tomorrow, we're going to pick out new furniture for the den. It's my job to pick—Mastercard or Visa."

He stares out the window, watching the brilliant red water shimmer in the sun. "I wish I could surf, even just for an hour."

I take a deep breath and tell him not to get mad. "You could come with us next time. We don't have to tell Skeezer, and you don't even have to talk to *him*," I say, not daring to say Adrian's name out loud.

"Are you in love with him or something?" Jim asks. Then he tells me to forget it. He doesn't want to know if his sister is in love with a Val. For a second, I consider telling him all about Adrian, Ava, and my father, but then I hear the floorboards groan and heavy steps pounding on the carpet.

Putting his finger to his lips, Jim smiles strangely, and gives me our secret handshake.

Later that night he's standing over my bed, trembling. I'm not sure how long he's been there.

"How does it feel to stand up? I can't remember."

"Once you paddle out, you'll remember," I say, scared. "It's like riding a bicycle."

When Jim falls asleep, I push my nightstand in front of the door to my bedroom to keep my mother out, take the phone into my closet, and call my father's service.

"Is this an emergency call?" the operator asks.

"Yes," I say, looking at Jim.

He is quiet now, breath falling softly, almost drowned out against the sound of the tide.

"I'm sorry, Dr. Mason is in France; it may take him a day or two to call you."

~~~

The next day, my mother has my bedroom door removed. A small guy with a tape measure comes and loosens the hinges, and it crashes down to the carpet.

"Too much hiding," she explains. "Too many secrets and late-night talking. Too much I don't understand."

My mother walks in and out of my room three times in a row.

"Doors encourage secrets, Medina. I am watching now. I do see."

She gives the handyman twenty dollars cash.

~~~

The air is muggy with smoke at 7:30 A.M. The scientists are already at Lunada Bay, wearing rubber masks and bacteria barriers. They dive in sealed suits, counting plankton with green machines, infrared lights flashing in the forest of seaweed. I stand above, on the cliffs, watching a camera crew pan over the burnt hillside, while a reporter interviews an arson expert.

"What clues do we have about the mind of an arsonist?" the reporter asks.

"Usually Caucasian males. Highly intelligent. Often sexually impotent," the expert says neutrally.

❧❧❧

When my father finally calls from Paris, the sound of the long-distance phone is like a train roaring.

"How are you guys holding up over there?" he asks. "Not that it's such a bad place to hold up in." Ha ha ha.

"Did you get my message?" I say quickly. "Jim needs you."

"Put him on then."

I tell my father that it isn't something that can be handled on the phone. I tell him he needs to come home immediately and talk to Jim face-to-face.

"Well," my father says, "I can't just hop on a plane, Medina. These conferences aren't for fun, they're a matter of life and death for millions of people."

He tells me to calm down and says admonishingly, "Look, I talked to your mother earlier. She said Jim was fine."

"He isn't," I say. "She's lying."

My father's voice is very smooth and soft now.

"Your mother told me the truth—it's you who's been acting out, Medina. You've got to stop fighting with your mother all the time."

He silences my protests. "I understand your anger; I'm very angry with her too, for different reasons. But we need to leave Jim out of it, hon."

༖༖༖

The next afternoon, Jim is on the couch, watching cartoons. There are Robinson's catalogues spread before him and over-sized UPS boxes in the hall, a few still unopened. There are packing peanuts scattered across the floor.

"Let's go out for the day, just you and me," I say. "There's a waterpark in the Torrance Mall where a machine makes fake waves in a pool."

I tell him to hurry, before my mother comes to stop us.

On the bus, we pass a bunch of surfers sitting on the cliffs, idle and bickering. A film of tide covers the water like the skin of old milk. Jim ducks, pulling me down with him. He huddles against the Naugahyde, shaking his head until we're out of the curve, afraid the guys will see how much he's changed.

"Oh man, oh man," he says over and over.

༖༖༖

The wave machine is shaped like a wheat thresher; it hums and clicks in the cavernous mall. The pool is Olympic sized, acrid with chlorine, bright blue with pictures of dolphins and starfish painted in glossy green along the bottom.

Valley kids stand along the sides, hopping from one foot to the other, gossiping among themselves, checking out girls who wear long feather earrings and pastel tube tops.

Jim and I each take plastic-coated numbers and pin them to our wet suits. No one else is wearing wet suits, only bright boardshorts with neon patches along the panels. Jim is looking around, lost, trying to be cool, wearing sunglasses, fidgeting.

Finally a man at an intercom calls a number; it's Jim's turn, but he tells me to go first.

The water feels like it's breathing, sucking me backward as the machine whirrs to a start. The wave is gentle, slow, short like a burp. I stand up easily, twisting around, trying to speed it up. I look at the fluorescent lights, smell the popcorn and chocolate cookies, hear another voice on an intercom advertising a sale at Sears. Then the water ducks down with a smushy slap, until I kneel to a finish. I hear the machine whirr for the next person.

"You better imagine you're somewhere else," I tell Jim, shrugging. He sighs, telling me he'll try. I watch him slide over the mechanical wave; he stands still, moving slowly, putting his arms out listlessly.

For ten dollars a ride, we decide that it isn't worth it to go again.

"Manhattan Beach would be cooler," I say, elbowing him.

"Surfing milk would be cooler," he says, ignoring me.

⌒⌒⌒

In the bus on the way home, Jim tells me he feels bad for all the kids at the mall.

"I thought you hated Vals," I say, looking at my nails before I bite them.

"It's the little kids I feel sorry for," he amends. "They don't know what real waves are like. Just that terrible recycled air, awful lighting, fake fish."

Then he's quiet for a while, thinking. He looks around to make sure no one's watching, swallows a few pills. "No wonder they grow up so weird."

He goes to sleep, his head on my lap. It's hard to wake him up when we get to our stop.

"Shhhh," he says. "I feel too tired to walk home." I tell him he can't sleep on the bus, shaking him until he gets up heavily, knocking an old lady in the head with his backpack. He tells her he's sorry, and starts to lie down on the floor. But I pull him up again, my heart beating fast.

That night he wakes me up at 2:00 A.M., thrashing loudly in his sleep, moaning about water, fire, and other stuff I don't understand.

"I'm okay," he says, when I wake him. "I shouldn't have taken the black ones with the white ones. I'm okay now, go away."

෨෨෨

Adrian wants me to come out and have dinner with him at Dave's Italian Restaurant. He's a vegetarian, and his favorite food is spaghetti with tomato sauce and green olives.

After dinner, we park the car a block away from my house. The street is deserted and dark, except for a light in my neighbor's window. Gulls sit on the Murphys' hedge, swaying in the breeze, ruffling their feathers, shooing away insects. Adrian puts his arm around me and kisses me, running his tongue along my teeth.

I climb over the gearshift onto his lap, kissing him back,

smelling licorice chapstick on his mouth. His hands cup my hipbones, then travel up and down my back, impeded only by the strap of my bra. The air is hot in the Mustang, but we can't crack the windows because of the smell outside.

"Take it off," I say, my voice very loud in the stillness.

He looks at the neighbor's lighted window, nervous. I tell him not to worry about it, everyone in Palos Verdes thinks I'm a slut anyway.

"Maybe we should fuck on their lawn, really freak them out." I laugh. Then I tell him I'm tired of having sex in the cramped car.

"We can't even roll around," I say, rubbing against him. "It would be more fun in a bed, free."

"We *could* go to my room," he says. But he tells me it can't be tonight, he has to study again. "We have to wait until finals are over."

I warn him we better do it soon, we don't have too much time before he goes away. I tell him he's going to have lots of older college girlfriends and forget me.

I tell him I'll never forget him, though.

છબ્જ

My father misses his next two calls, so I leave a message with his service to call me on Thursday. I stay home all evening, sitting near the phone, but the warm dry winds knock the phone lines down.

At midnight I'm chewing my nails, looking out the slats of the venetian blinds at the waves of flame that consume dry brush above. The newest fire is close to a group of houses on Crystal Cove. The firefighters evacuate terrified citizens and hose down the horse stables with foamy flame retardant.

"No way," Jim says, tears springing to his eyes. "Not the horses!"

All night he sleeps in a sleeping bag on the floor in my room.

My mother sits down, half inside my door, strangely mellow, staring at him for a long time. Her eyes are wide like a doll's when she looks at me.

∽∽∽

One of the bottomfeeders stops by the next day, introducing himself to my mother, casually asking if Jim's around. My mother lies.

"Jim's not here right now, Josh, is it? But I have a question for you."

She asks if Josh has noticed anything strange about Jim lately.

Even though he's a bottomfeeder, Josh is polite to a mother.

"No, nothing, nothing strange," Josh says.

"What a frightening boy," she says to me when Josh leaves. "He isn't your Valley boyfriend, is he?"

∽∽∽

"Tell Jimbo he owes us," one of the bottomfeeders calls as I walk past Pratt Point. They've been living in a green army tent, six or seven of them, two hundred yards from the water, smoking heroin, waiting for the tide to subside.

I creep near the mouth of the tent, cringing at the smell,

afraid. The bottomfeeders are lying together on the floor of the tent in a pool of sand and garbage, laughing together, pointing at a sandcrab running in circles on a paper plate.

"Come in, Medina, maybe we can work something out. Your brother owes us, big time," Josh says, picking dead skin from his feet, flicking it at the corner of the tent.

"Yeah," Doogie says, "we could give him a discount, or something."

He rubs his crotch, like he's itching it, and lunges for me, but stumbles and falls against Damian, who pushes him off and screams.

"You asshole, you broke my fucking leg."

As I run from the tent, I hear a scuffle and laughter, and a moan when someone hits someone else on the head with a stick.

Janie Tricot started going to Pratt Point last year. All of a sudden she had long hair on her legs. Then she started in with the rambling Jesus speeches. After her escape from Palos Verdes Hospital, the cops found Janie in a bus, curled in a fetal position, stoned out of her mind, in possession of heroin. She scratched the first cop who tried to walk her off the bus. She stabbed the second with a barrette. The Tricots settled out of court, Janie went through rehabilitation. Her parents paid a ten-thousand-dollar fine.

Now Janie walks with her mother each afternoon at four, her eyes dulled with lithium, her mouth slack like a hound's. Mrs. Tricot always smiles at the neighbors.

"Just fine," she calls as she waves at them pleasantly.

～～～

"Oh come on, grouchy, smile," my mother says to Jim. "I have a surprise for you."

Five new packages have arrived today on Via Neve, each addressed to Mrs. Phil Mason.

"Open that one, Jimmy."

Jim raises his fist, punching the air, not moving. He is sarcastic.

"Go on, Mom, you open it. Take the bastard to the cleaners."

"But they're for you, that one's good, open it." My mother points, nodding.

But Jim knows who they're really meant for.

"Get every last cent, Mom," he says, forgetting to smile.

～～～

There's a present for me, too, in an elongated box next to my bed. Pinprick airholes are punched into the cardboard. I hear rustling sounds coming from inside.

At first I don't see the tortoises. Then I notice a brownish lump pressed against the far end. It has brilliant stains and markings on its back, some star-shaped, some abstract. Its head is gone, terrified, in retreat from the light.

LIVE ANIMALS—HANDLE WITH CARE is stenciled on the right side of the box. I open the other end and see the other tortoise. Scooping the smaller one into my hand, I smell its musty odor and pet its cold shell, cleaning its droppings with wet newspaper. I hold it close, bringing it to the living room to show it to Jim.

My mother is looking out the bay window, her eyes narrowed, shredding a tissue in her fingers. Before I can leave unnoticed, she turns around.

"Thank you for the tortoises," I say, wary.

"They're from Jim," she says. "It was his idea."

I turn to leave, hoping to escape quickly, but my mother's voice stops me at the front door. She tells me Jim's been distant and increasingly strange to her lately. Laughing inappropriately, ignoring her when she talks.

Moving slowly, she comes toward me and warns me not to try to turn Jim against her. Then she touches my arm. "Promise me you won't. Please, Medina. I'll buy you a new wet suit."

For the first time in years she looks straight at me. I pull away.

අආආ

After dinner on Thursday, Jim lights up a cigarette in the den, tapping the ashes into his third-grade soccer trophy.

"I don't want smoking in this house, Jim," my mother tells him softly.

"Aye, aye, captain," he says, going outside.

Jim takes the red-and-white package of cigarettes to the pool. He sits on the step in the shallow end of the pool, lighting match after match, throwing them into the far end. I watch, hesitant, leaning against the rail on the edge of the stairs. He lights a cigarette with his last match. He doesn't inhale exactly, he sucks at the filter, half-swallows the smoke, then loudly forces it out of his nose.

"If you're gonna smoke, do it right," I call out, teasing him.

He looks up at me, moonlight illuminating his face. His

eyes are sunken, ringed with black, like a skull. With his shirt off, I can see the protruding ridge of bones across his back, the splotchy bruises on his arms, how thin he's become. He lays his head on his board, and begins sobbing, a low, steady rumble.

"Oh my God, what's wrong with you," I say, running toward him, wading in with my clothes on.

"Dad wrote a secret letter to Mom. She wasn't supposed to tell me about it yet."

He twitches, trembling in the nervous air, whacking the water in rage.

"They're dividing us up. You're going to be living the lux life with him soon. He says he doesn't want me."

He looks up at me, haunted, his jaw clenched tight.

"Dad thinks I'm exactly like Mom." Then he tells me he doesn't know who he's like anymore.

⧞⧞⧞

"Give me Dad's letter," I tell my mother, wet, fists clenched.

"I'm not sure where I put it," she says vaguely, not looking up from her movie magazine.

I upturn the trash can in the kitchen, searching frantically through tuna cans and refried beans stuck to wet plastic. Then I kick over the trash cans in the living room and the foyer.

"Where did you throw it?" I scream at her.

"Stop making such a mess," she says, calm.

I use a garden shovel to tip the huge mechanical trash bin on its side in the front yard, waving away flies and moths, gagging. I say "Hola" to the maid who watches from the neighbor's window and pull plastic bags over my hands while I furiously dig.

I come in empty-handed to face my mother.

"I don't believe Dad wrote any letter," I tell her.

"Ask him," she says, calmly flipping the page.

Something clatters outside. Then she looks up. Jim emerges from the pool, creeping past the back stairs, sneaking down the trail that leads to Pratt Point. She's too slow to catch him.

☙☙☙

It's Saturday night. My mother looks me up and down, arching an eyebrow.

"Look at you, whoo-weee, a black dress with pearls. Elegant, girl. Your father would like that."

She points at my face.

"There must be a very special boy in your life, if there's lipstick involved."

"He's just a guy, Mom. A nice guy."

"Is he a surfer? One of those young boys from below?" She gestures at the ocean under the window. "Is he the tall one with long hair?"

"No, Mom, he has short hair. We're only friends."

My mother peers intently, smacking her lips.

"Lipstick isn't just friends, little girl, and neither is that outfit you've got on tonight."

Jim walks in, pupils very large, sniffing the air.

"Toilet water?" he says, grinning weakly.

As he settles into the couch, clicking to a war movie on the television, I try to catch his eye.

"Stop winking at your brother," my mother says.

Jim twitches. "Mom, lay off her, okay?"

My mother comes toward him, but he steps back as if in pantomime. She starts to protest, but he turns up the volume on the television. Heroic military music fills the room as German soldiers lie in wait for a young American GI on the screen.

Suddenly Jim jumps at me, knocking over the magazine rack, sending *National Geographics* flying through the air. As we begin to wrestle, my mother pouts.

"Stop it."

I'm laughing, unsteady on the high heels. Jim trips me, pinning me to the floor, easily holding me down, tickling me wildly as I writhe.

"Try to get away," he repeats over and over, pressing too hard.

My mother is pretending to join in, laughing as she tries to separate us with her hand. Jim slaps out at her playfully, knocking her down.

"We're just clowning around, Mom. Don't get jealous."

The hairs rise on the back of my neck. My mother sucks in air. We all stop laughing. The only sound comes from the blaring television, where a battle is now in full swing.

The Germans have captured the American soldier. As he looks for an escape route his eyes dart back and forth.

"I'm not *jealous,* Jim," my mother says, wounded, backing up on her hands on the carpet.

He rises, staring into her eyes, gritting his teeth. "Yes you are, you're jealous of anyone who comes near me."

"Jim!" she cries out in surprise, her eyes round black Os.

A few uncomfortable seconds go by.

"Mom, I can't stay with you all the time. I want to go out and have some fun with my sister."

My mother turns very white. She starts to choke and fan herself with a magazine.

"I thought we *were* having fun together. You said we were."

She clutches at her heart, gurgling all of a sudden. "I, well, Jim . . ."

Jim takes her fluttering hand, holding it limply, his eyes flickering with rage and defeat. My mother smiles uncertainly, then puts her hand over his. We all watch the television as the GI is airlifted away.

My mother freezes, a smile rising and falling. She says she wants us all to stay together tonight. She says it's high time we had a family night. She clicks the channel changer.

Jim suddenly drops her hand and runs out of the house.

A horn sounds.

〜〜〜

"You look beautiful," Adrian says in the car. "Wow."

I kiss him, brushing carpet fibers off my dress, smoothing my hair.

"Let's go somewhere special tonight. Finals are over," he says.

"I know just the place."

My father's house is cavernous, the ceilings are arched like a medieval church. I tiptoe through his white living room, his Chinese lacquered furniture. I sit down at an oak table for twelve.

"Did my dad say anything about me coming to live here?"

"No."

"He hasn't called us in two weeks. My mother says he wants to split me and Jim up." I glare at the shiny silver candlesticks.

Then I say, "I'd never live here," but I'm thinking of the shabby furniture at the house on Via Neve, the corduroy couch, thick with dog hairs, the rickety rattan, the scratched tables.

I run a paper clip over the smooth antique table, leaving a scratch.

Adrian sits close, watching for a moment, then takes the paper clip and smiles. He draws a thin line next to mine.

"Now it's official," he says.

"Some maid will buff it out. Now for the fun part—where's the master bedroom?"

"You're crazy," Adrian says.

We climb the spiral staircase to my father's bedroom; I jump on his mountain range of pillows, pulling it apart, ripping it.

"They've got a beautiful bed."

"Yeah."

"Are there millions hidden under the mattress?" I ask, laughing carefully.

"No," he says. "They hide money in a fake cantaloupe in the refrigerator."

I giggle with him and punch the rose silk bedspread. I throw Turkish pillows against the wall until the feathers eddy on the air-conditioned breeze. I kick over the table, shattering a glass vase.

"This is fun," I say, "isn't it?"

"Sure," he says, uneasily.

"My father won't want me now," I say.

I pull him on top of me, kissing him. We roll around for a few minutes, running our hands over each other's bumpy, hot clothes. Then he turns over, lights my father's candles, switches off the lamp. Looking me in the eye, he pulls my sweater over my head, but the buttons gets stuck in my hair. I tell him to close his eyes. Then I strip down, naked.

"Okay, open them," I say, turning around slowly so he can see. He looks at my body, biting his lip. Then he strips, too, and stands in front of me.

"I like your arms," I tell him, feeling the smooth tricep muscles with my hands.

When we lie down on my father's bed, Adrian takes my hand, guides it down. I tell him I've never done oral sex before, but I want to try it on him. I tell him I'll go slow, not to move.

"I won't," he promises, closing his eyes, waiting. I kiss his stomach, laughing when his muscles quiver, feeling his body rise up.

I look at his face to see if I'm doing it right. His eyes are wide open, his mouth moving, hurrying me on. When I choke he slows down, grabbing my hair, pulling it hard. The candles flicker in a sudden rush of air and I see a framed photograph of my father in Hawaii on the nightstand. Looking at it, I pull my mouth away. I sit up, pulling in my elbows, covering my breasts with my arms.

Adrian looks up, noticing me look at the photograph. He's breathing hard, then he rolls onto his stomach away from me.

He tells me to turn the damn photograph over.

We listen to a siren move past.

"Let's go to your room," I say, breaking the silence.

∽∽∽

Adrian drops me off at eleven. There's a beach towel hanging over my brother's window so I can't see in. I throw pebbles at it until he opens the window just a crack, then tells me the bottomfeeders are harassing him for the money he owes. They're coming to his window, rattling it, making threats.

At midnight, the bottomfeeders are lying in the army tent in a cloud of smoke. There is loud music coming from the corner, metal thrashing sounds. I hover a few feet from the opening of the tent and call out, "Hey, Simm, how much does Jim owe?"

"I can't hear you," Simm says. "Come in."

"I said," I shout, "how much fucking money?"

Josh comes to the mouth of the tent, pulling his long hair from his eyes.

"Look, it's Medina Mason." He makes a sarcastic face. "How do you do?" Then he laughs, and says, "I know how you do, I've heard you're pretty good."

"Here." I throw sixty dollars in tens and fives into the tent, and then step back.

Josh comes out, looking at the cash, spitting at my feet, thrashing around to the music, singing. Spitting again. "Punk rock is cool," he says and laughs.

"You're a homo, Josh," Simm says. "Sixty isn't gonna cut it, Medina, he owes at least one fifty."

"Please leave Jim alone. I'll bring more later, but this is all I've got saved," I tell him.

Simm looks at my legs. "That isn't all you've got."

∽∽∽

There are no fires for a few days. Life goes on as usual.

My mother tags the family furniture, plastic sheets it for removal. She happily signs the waivers, releasing it. After a week, a van pulls up with new furniture—light oak, Italian marble. New rugs are softly wheeled in. My mother signs and signs.

"It's almost perfect now," she tells Jim. "We'll have a beautiful house, better than his."

"I'm not going to steal from Dad anymore," Jim says.

"I can't hear you," she says, shushing him.

Our family portrait is back in its space over the fireplace, except someone is missing. In his place is the family pug dog, beautifully rendered. My brother and I, on either side of the dog, are separated by an unnatural gap, because Puggles isn't quite big enough to fill the space between us.

My father still hasn't called.

✐✐✐

Jim is sitting in the backyard when I come home from the store. He tells me he doesn't want to go inside; he's afraid of the bottomfeeders. He says the house is evil now, dark and hot, full of plastic and packing chemicals.

"I hate all that new stuff," he says. "It smells horrible."

I think for a while, then tell him I have an idea.

"We can take the old tent out of the garage," I say. "We'll set it up right here, live in the backyard until Dad comes home."

"Dad won't let me live with him." I tell him he's wrong, and I can prove it.

"How?" he asks hopefully. Then I tell him I'll bet my surfboard. Then he knows I'm telling the truth. He's suddenly energetic, full of plans.

"We don't even have to go inside to use the bathroom, we'll just rough it in the yard like we're camping, tell ghost stories at night," he says.

But when we go to the garage, the tent is gone. The shelves are empty except for my sleeping bag and Jim's old bike. Even the paddle machine has vanished. My mother has given all the old stuff to Goodwill.

⮑⮑⮑

"Card number 234-237-116-221 has been canceled," a catalog operator tells my mother when she tries to order a color television for Jim.

"What do you mean?" my mother says. "I'm Mrs. Phil Mason."

The operator says, "Your card is void. Until Mr. Phil Mason reinstates you, Visa cannot authorize your use of the card."

"But it's important," my mother insists. Then she tries again. "I also have a Mastercard."

When the operator comes back on the line, he tells my mother the Mastercard has been canceled, too.

"Who'll pay?" she cries, kicking the leg of the couch, cracking it.

⮑⮑⮑

Starfish can grow new legs. If you break four legs off, they might grow six back. Many have survived in the red tide pools until this week, but even they are beginning to wash up on the beach.

The remaining members of the Palos Verdes Key Club mobilize, wearing gauze masks and full-body rain gear.

They scoop the tenacious orange creatures off the rocks with garden shovels, sometimes breaking off a leg or two, and put them in Ziploc bags for transport to Laguna Beach. A battalion of Mercedes sedans and station wagons waits on Via Neve, back seats carefully coated with plastic sheeting against leaks.

In the closest tide pool, a Fish and Game Department scientist demonstrates "proper relocation procedure." Tennis ladies giggle as they practice, neatly applying starfish to wet granite, as if gluing on Halloween decorations.

"Come on, stick, stick," Harriet House says, mashing a starfish enthusiastically onto a tide pool rock, coaching it. "You gotta stick, little guy."

As the cars drive away in a line, Jim and I stand in the driveway, waving to the neighbors. My mother watches from the window, crouched back a bit. A police car slowly cruises toward us, then stops. My mother bangs on the window, motioning for us to come inside. She opens the screen, calling out our names, telling us to come to her immediately.

"Is everything okay over here?" the cop says. Jim stands, frozen. I nod, confused. My mother is frantic now, she's yelling for the cop to get off our driveway.

"Do you have a search warrant?" she yells. "You can't come on my property without a search warrant!"

The policeman turns to Jim and me, then we hear a crash. My mother is throwing ashtrays and plates out the window, shouting at the cop, telling him she'll call the FBI if he doesn't get off our driveway immediately.

The cop takes a breath, then lets it out slowly. Turning to leave, he shakes his head, tired.

"Your father called us from France. He asked us to check on you, because he can't get through on the phone."

"He's lying," my mother says. "There haven't been any calls at all."

※※※

The fire tonight is at Dapplegray Down. Someone sees a man run away from the flames. He is described as Tall. Mexican. Fast. A posse of citizens surrounds the peninsula each night. But the arsonist knows how to evade them.

As Adrian and I watch the flames, I tell him Jim's in big trouble; he isn't eating anything and he's taking lots of pills.

"I need money," I say. "I want you to get the money out of the fake cantaloupe in my father's refrigerator."

"You're acting like he killed someone," Adrian says, serious.

On the way home, we pass a guy hiding in the bushes near my house. He's sitting on a backpack, eyes glinting red in the headlights.

I don't tell Adrian it's my brother.

※※※

My mother locked all the doors again tonight. Even my sliding glass door. I throw pebbles at Jim's window, but he's gone. I wait outside, face pressed to the glass, breathing in swirls, writing him a message in a fog of breath.

I have to talk to you.

I go to sleep in the garden inside my tan Big Five sleeping bag from the garage, watching silvery snails circle the wet ferns and the leaves of the eucalyptus tree flash in the moonlight. The air is blowing from the south, mixing the smell of red tide with salt and ash. I crawl into the bottom part of the bag, hoping the snails can't reach me.

⌁⌁⌁

In the middle of the night, Jim wakes me up by sitting on my head.

"Where were you?" I say, pushing him off. "Gross."

"Shhhh. Come to the pool."

Jim is dirty, red-eyed, lighting matches and throwing the lit ones toward the deep end.

"I saw you in the bushes," I say. "Were you waiting for me?"

"You've been right about Mom," he says in a deep, strange voice. "I'm sorry I didn't believe you."

For the next half hour he stays silent, smoking, paddling from end to end of the dirty, heated water on a surfboard. I swim next to him with a diver's flashlight, guiding his way. He takes the flashlight, gets out of the water and throws it at the moon.

When he finally speaks again, his voice cracks, he says he can't believe she's been lying all this time. He wants to kill her. "I can't stop thinking about killing her.

"Are you afraid of me now?" he asks, shivering, not looking at me.

"No," I say, kissing him. "And I know you're the arsonist."

I say this casually, as if speaking about the temperature of water.

⤳⤳⤳

"Get up," Jim whispers just before sunrise, gently splashing me awake from a nervous sleep. The tortoises are asleep on the deck, burrowed in their box.

My mother struggles down the steps, yawning. She has her hand on her hip, looking past me to Jim in the deep end.

"What are you doing out here?" she calls out.

"Looking at the stars," I say, quickly.

"Counting them," Jim yells, "one, two, three, four." He laughs bitterly. "There are so many stars, it takes all night to count them."

"What? What?" my mother says, coming to the edge of the pool.

"Don't come any further, or you might drown," Jim yells, splashing her lightly until she squeals.

"She's meeellllting," he cries out, splashing her again, imitating the wicked witch in the Wizard of Oz.

His eyes glitter dangerously. His cigarette smolders. The first slice of sun glimmers through the blackness.

⤳⤳⤳

There are only a few sentences about pyromaniacs in the book I borrowed from the library, *Abnormal Psychology*. All of them fit.

"Pyromaniacs are secretive and evasive. Even those closest to them are often strangers to their secrets. Pyromania, like any of the mania-class disorders, is a serious illness —it is always difficult to stop the patient's obsessive thought patterns from reoccurring. In some cases impossible . . ."

⬿⬿⬿

I write him a letter, shove it under his door.

> *Jim,*
> *We better stick together now.*
> *Please take me with you when you go out at night.*
> *We're a tribe, no matter what.*
> *Love, me.*

While I wait for him to come back, I concentrate on cutting out pictures from *Surfer* magazine, making a collage of all the lush, beautiful places beyond Palos Verdes: Hawaii, Bali, Java, Australia. I'm going to give the collage to Jim for our birthday, so he'll imagine the places we can run to.

There's a picture of Frieda Zane on a wave in Eccles, Australia. She's crouched low on the board for balance, her arms barely raised off the water, skimming. Even though the wave is as big as an apartment building, she's riding through it, smiling, navigating its power with calm, graceful finesse.

"It's not impossible," I say out loud, rehearsing what I'm going to tell Jim. "We'll get out of here, no matter how hard it looks."

I know my brother will forget about fire, once he remembers about water.

⬿⬿⬿

At 5:00 A.M. that morning I find Jim on the floor, hidden from view, burrowed under blankets and books. The tortoises are loose, under the sheets with him. I pound on his shoulder softly, afraid when he won't move. He emerges after a while rubbing his eyes, looking at me as if I were very far away. His hair is tangled, unwashed, crumpled in snaky coils.

"Room service?"

"Jim, don't make jokes, because I'm serious. I think we should do what Jody Ferguson did."

Jody Ferguson, age thirteen, hit herself with a paperweight and scraped her knees and face on the sidewalk. Then she went to the school counselor, showed him the welts, the bruises, the scrapes. She told him it was her dad that hit her. She never told them what her father *really* did, but she wrote a letter to Janie Tricot, explaining everything.

Her dad used to touch her at night, when her mother went to sleep. He touched her in places fathers should never touch.

After Jody went to the counselor, the police moved very quickly.

Within twenty-four hours she was living in another state in a group home. A place beyond the reach of her parents.

"We could do that," I whisper matter-of-factly. "You can do the same thing, then I'll run away, too. No one would ever know about the fires."

"No," Jim says after a while, shaking his head. He sighs, hoisting a tortoise onto his chest, running his hand over its smooth shell. It pokes its head out and then pulls back quickly.

"Why not?" I ask, still whispering.

"I'm finished with lying."

I hear a noise in the bush, so I dive low. When an opossum crawls past, I relax again. "There's another way. We could stay together if we do it."

I tell him there's money hidden at our father's house. I

say I'll steal it and we can run away to Hawaii. "We can always repay it later." I give him the collage, and he looks at it, tears in his eyes.

"But what about the thing you said about tribes?" he asks.

"Which thing?"

"If you leave, you die. Period."

"We're our own tribe," I say. "Just me and you."

Jim thinks. He says he'll never escape this place. But he says he's in anyway. We do the secret handshake, then I crawl under his blanket and fall back into an exhausted sleep, smiling.

"Don't smile when you sleep, it's bad luck," Jim warns, shaking me.

❧❧❧

The Dixons are the only family on Via Neve. They don't go to Mexico or Hawaii because their son is on a dialysis machine for his kidneys.

Tonight, Mrs. Dixon sits on the porch fanning herself with a Chinese screened fan, wearing a scarf over her nose, toasting the air. She holds the glass up to us as I walk past.

"Here's to the tide turning!" she says, jubilant.

❧❧❧

My mother is baking cookies. The smell of red tide is almost overpowered by the scent of melting chocolate and butter. Jim is staring at my mother as she bustles around.

"They'll be ready in a minute," she tells Jim. "They're special for your birthday."

"They're burning, Mom, can't you smell it?" Jim says.

"Sweetie, they aren't burning at all, they are almost ready."

She is shoveling out crisp, golden brown Toll House cookies onto the countertop with a spatula when Jim douses them with a full bottle of beer.

"Why do you burn everything?" Jim asks.

⌒⌒⌒

He's in his room now, sitting on his bed, listening to soft music in the dark. When I knock on his door, he sticks his head out, saying, "Shhh. I'm packing."

I see his wet suit in the trash can, and his favorite board-shorts, too.

"You better take your wet suit," I say. "I'm sure you'll need it."

He shakes his head, no. Then he hugs me and pushes me out the door.

⌒⌒⌒

At the end of the driveway, Jim is uncoiling a length of rope. His backpack is open. The tortoises are in the inner pocket, each wrapped in a towel. In the outer pouch is lighter fluid and a bottle of Bacardi 151.

"You know what Mom gave me as a gift?" Jim asks.

I don't answer, because I'm looking at the rope, scared.

"Look at this."

He takes out a perfect square-cut diamond; it flashes in

the dark. Then he looks out at the ocean. "See ya," he says calmly, throwing the diamond far over the cliff. When he picks up the lighter fluid, I grab his hand.

"We don't have to burn anything. Let's just run for it like we planned."

"Did you ever think that I had a plan, all by my stupid, slow, idiot self? Or do you think only you can come up with plans?"

Water and fire sound the same when they hiss. The coil of rope curls and cracks when Jim strikes the pack of matches and lights the end, as if he's going to light a cigarette. It bursts into flame, and he throws it toward the dry festuca grass, a snake on fire. The grass goes up in flame as he laughs and beats his stomach with the small of his hand.

"It's over, it's really over," he whispers, lighting a match, burning another piece of snaky rope.

As the fire begins, Jim breathes deeply, closing his eyes.

I crouch low, ready to run, watching a bush burn. Coils of orange rope are wrapped around my brother's neck like African beads.

"You promise we'll stick together," I say, the hair rising on my neck.

"Sorry, Medina, I'm not going to promise anyone anything ever again." He throws the bottle of Bacardi high into the air, until it breaks on the grass and ignites; then he giggles into his hand.

"Run, run, run, as fast as you can, genius, get fucking out of here." He kisses me quickly on the mouth, and takes off down the trail to the beach. The eucalyptus begins to bend, the fuchsias melt in orange streaks. The flames rise and snap.

I sprint down the trail, through wind, fire, and water, the smell of fish in my nose, following my brother, slipping on seaweed. Lodged in the rocks are silvery bonito, dead but still shining. Stars fall, a flicker, smoke, blackness, then another flicker.

I crash through muddy tide pools, calling my brother's name, ducking from a frenzy of seagulls flapping past to circle the fire.

"Faster," Jim calls. "I'll race you." He leads by twenty feet. I fall and get up again. Jim stops, watching me get up, then throws a pebble, giggling, looking up into the sky.

He yells, cupping his mouth like a megaphone, "Hey, see that star? That's my present to you. Happy birthday."

I hear his feet running on the sand, then he stops to shake the tortoises out of his backpack gently. He runs again.

"Wait," I shout, running into the dark, and falling over another rock.

But Jim is beyond my reach.

❧❧❧

They use special machines to clean the sands of Palos Verdes, yellow tractors that thresh, mix, and spit out the crystals into fine, white powder. It is one of these machines that finds Jim, facedown, at Helsa Cove, five miles beyond Angel Point. Naked, stripped bare, wet, with a faint red welt on his back and kidney area.

The driver of the Sand Machine grabs a stick from the front cab, a stick usually used for fighting off stray dogs.

Today he uses the stick to turn Jim over. Jim grumbles and then screams at the man.

The man uses his radio to call base, and they send backup, another yellow Sand Machine, with another bewildered driver with a dog stick.

Jim tries to rise, but falls back into the sand, mumbling incoherently about sunsets and motherfuckers and fire. His eyes are freshly sown with Pratt Point acid. His arms scratch at the sky, trying to turn it off as it lightens to daylight.

"My God! It's Jim Mason, that kid from Via Neve . . ."

The backup driver, a surfer from Lunada Point, moves fast, panicking.

"Call the police. I'll stay here with him."

Jim is picked up by the police and placed carefully in a white van, whisked away to Palos Verdes Mental Health Clinic, which isn't in Palos Verdes at all. Later they take him to Camarillo State Hospital for the criminally insane. He gives the television camera a hang-loose sign as he leaves. "See ya," he says.

"Suspected Palos Verdes Arsonist Nabbed," the papers say.

In the hospital, my mother corners a nervous young nurse, telling him to call all the best hotels in Europe, certain that he can find Phil Mason.

Instead, the nurse asks questions. He asks if Jim has been smoking cocaine regularly, and how often he's been taking methamphetamines. My mother is silent for a moment, rocking back and forth in her chair.

"You better let me see him," my mother finally says. "He needs me."

Soon after, the Palos Verdes police come to ask questions, badges glittering, mouths moving slowly.

"Did you ever see him start a fire?" they ask us.

"Never," my mother cuts in quickly.

"Did he have a chronic cocaine problem, or an addiction of any kind?" the police probe kindly.

"He took a few pills, smoked a little pot," I tell them, exhausted. "But those weren't the problem."

•

Salt

∾∾∾

•

I live in Santa Barbara now at Gate School, the best girls' school in California, two hours north of Palos Verdes. When my father returned, he sent me here, giving me a gold card, crying, kissing me again and again.

I have new clothes, a silver pen, a leather backpack. They sit in the closet, while I wear my brother's old clothes. I pull his big wet suit on, standing on the sand, wrapping duct tape around the legs and arms for insulation.

The water is colder in Santa Barbara, murkier, blacker. I try to feel the old rush of motion, but I always end up near the shore.

༄༅༅

Jim wasn't a good arsonist. The house on Via Neve is still standing. Only the fuchsias and the eucalyptus trees burned, plus half of the old palm. The new gardener is replacing them.

A few more fires happened before they caught the real pyromaniac, a local forty-two-year-old structural engineer. A weekend volunteer in the fire-watch posse.

"Starting fires is beautiful, almost spiritual," he said in his confession. "People run around like ants, while I just stand back and watch them."

Marge Paxton gave an interview to the *Times*. "He seemed like such a nice man. He always brought good wine to our barbecues."

His daughter wouldn't give an interview, but they photographed her as she tried to leave her house. I barely recognized the frightened expression on her face.

I knew her as a towel girl.

◅◦◦◦◦▻

The doctors call my brother's escape plan a severe schizophrenic break, aggravated by drug-induced psychosis. They say schizophrenia is encoded into a person's DNA, the same way eye color and hair color are. They have books to show my father and articles to prove their points. They have drugs to control violent outbursts. They have drugs for everything. Prozac, Zocolac, Xanax, Hanalax. All Jim's medicines rhyme.

He doesn't even try to stand up now. He is accustomed to falling. Each of his medications has its purpose, one to stop his thoughts, one to level his mood, one to counter the depressive feeling of having no mood. Another to counter the one that lifts him.

When I come to visit, I ask Jim how he's doing.

He says "Fuck." Then he says nothing for an hour.

As he sleeps, I watch his mouth move.

He won't see my mother at all.

◅◦◦◦◦▻

Almost every day my mother calls me at Gate School with news of diagnoses, tests, meds.

"He's on lithium salts now and four others. If you wait," she tells me, "I'll get you the names."

She asks me what electroshock therapy entails. I tell her.

She says, "No, no, they will not put those things all over my boy."

And yet they do. Cables and plungers and electric currents. Trial and error. That's what they use. But nothing works.

"If he dies," she says on my answering machine, "I'm going to go into the garage, put the door down . . ." I unplug the machine.

I visit my brother every week, but he doesn't look like my brother anymore. He is dry like a sea urchin shell, scooped out.

His face begins to bloat, lose its chin and cheekbones. His hair begins to fall out, his walk is slow and heavy.

When they move him to the lockdown ward, I try to make him laugh. I imitate Bugs Bunny and then Skeezer's weird whiny voice. Jim doesn't even smile. He looks through me, tells me to be careful of becoming a *harlot*. I don't understand how a surfer from Palos Verdes could come up with such words. Then I see the open book in his room. My brother is reading the Bible.

"If you look back," he says, "you turn into salt."

〜〜〜

"Girlie. Fuck me. Baby. Blondie."

They say this, the patients, as I walk down sea-green corridors with a burly male nurse.

"Don't listen to them," the nurse whispers, "just keep walking."

"Why is everyone here so crude?" I ask him.

"This is a hospital for the truly insane," he says. "It ain't no Palos Verdes garden party."

❦❦❦

Outside the hospital, I wait for the bus. A pomegranate tree, heavy fruit hanging low, sways in the hot Santa Ana winds. Large red balls fall from the flailing branches.

My brother stands in the window looking at me, screaming into the sun as it sets, pounding on the glass.

"Don't leave me here, Medina," he yells, "I'll burn."

The orderlies inject something into him, take him away.

The last time I see him, my brother smiles at me with a full mouth of acrylic teeth. The teeth click when he talks, like the doctor's shoes on the wide, white floors. Jim bashed out his real teeth on the side of the bed in a fit of rage. His rages are supposed to be controlled by medication, but sometimes he hides the pills in his cheek, only pretending to swallow. Then the rages come again, swift and merciless.

"I might leave this place soon," Jim says, as we stand by the electric door. "I feel very peaceful now."

Then he tells me to say good-bye to the Bayboys for him, he says he'll miss the big, winter waves. He's never going back to Palos Verdes, he says, but he doesn't want to come to Santa Barbara either.

"It sounds like a good place, but I'm going somewhere better."

He smiles at me when the orderly comes, the teeth clean and large, too big for his mouth.

"Good-bye." He waves. "I'm going to the moon."

He dies a few days later, overdosing on medications culled from other patients carefully, for months. He's stored them in his pants, in a crease he had taped together for this purpose. He dies smiling, relieved after so much waiting.

·

Stars

ᔧᔧᔧ

·

"It doesn't matter," I tell my parents, shaking my head.

My mother and father are making plans in the moonlight for a burial at sea, a reception, a long, heartfelt eulogy.

I say to them, "Who cares what kind of sandwiches? Who cares what shape the urn is?"

My mother tears a napkin into shreds. Her face is white, her hair loose and unkempt, graying at the roots suddenly. "Medina, we have to give him a good funeral at least." Then she says she can't believe her son is truly dead.

"What about his life, isn't that the point anyway?" I ask her.

⌐⌐⌐⌐

The surfers of Palos Verdes surround the floating ashes in a perfect arc in the water, holding hands, repeating words the priest drones on the boat. They stay silent, heads bowed, religious for a moment, bobbing like toy ducks.

I don't go to the funeral. I watch from the shore at Lunada Bay with binoculars, wearing a fancy green dress, counting all the surfers I know.

Later, the surfers come to the shabby house, where white paint is peeling off in long, weather-beaten strips. They tell me how sorry they are, how much they loved my brother. How the waves of Palos Verdes will never be the same without him.

I change into Jim's big, soft clothes, looking out the window.

The waves are the same, exactly.

꘎꘎꘎

Distant relatives from New York City are gathered in front of the buffet table; I recognize some of them from pictures. "You've grown so much," my aunt says, holding me away from her body, sniffling. "The last time I saw you, you were both just babies."

"I don't remember you," I tell her.

My mother is sobbing to everyone gathered around the catered finger sandwiches. "Maybe I made mistakes with my boy, but I *lived* for him."

I stare at her, shaking my head, laughing with no sound coming out. Acid bile rises up my throat.

"What do I do now?" my mother cries, collapsing into a ball on the floor.

"I'm leaving," I say. "Jim wouldn't even have liked this."

All the relatives hum around her like bees, encircling her protectively, as they move away from me.

"Oh, Sandy . . ." my aunt says. "She doesn't mean it. We're all upset today."

My mother cries on the couch, slumped over, "Oh, God, how could he have done this?"

"Whichever way felt the best," I tell myself, meaning it.

꘎꘎꘎

My father wants to give me every advantage now. He offers money, clothes, college.

"I don't want those things," I tell him gently.

A week later he sends me a self-help book called *Grieving.* The jacket cover is smooth and pale green like pond water. When I try to read the first chapter the words seem to float, half crazy like gibberish.

He visits me many times in my small, white, single dormitory room, where we step around the tortoises, step around the years.

"Your mother is almost a recluse now. There's trash heaped in piles all over the house," he says. "The neighbors want to call the health department."

I tell my father I don't want to think about that. I want to start over here, clean.

"Are you happy with this, Medina?" he asks, looking around at the small desk, the bare walls, the sandy wet suit on the bed, the wrinkled wet towels strung over the heater.

Later, he stands on the beach, waving, while I surf in the morning chill.

"*Happy Birthday,*" Adrian writes me from college near Sacramento, a few hours north of here. He's working in an animal hospital as a certified veterinary assistant four days a week. I imagine him sitting alone in a small room, looking into small furry carcasses to see what went wrong.

"*There are so many things that can go wrong,*" he writes, "*and a vet can't fix them all. But animals can't talk, so we have to guess. Sometimes I stay up all night, guessing. I try to help. Still, some of them die. In my hands.*"

∽∽∽

My mother calls a few weeks later from a motel in the Mojave Desert, far away from Palos Verdes. She explains she has nothing to lose now, she left the house with nothing, wearing only the yellow bathrobe. She had been sitting in the garage with the door down, but instead of waiting, she pressed down the pedal, drove straight through the wooden frame without stopping.

"For a minute," she says on the phone, "I was sure I would die."

My mother likes the emptiness of the desert. She's going to wait for my father to sell the house on Via Neve and then take the money and buy a little place near Joshua Tree National Monument. She says Joshua trees smell like salt when you rub their leaves with your fingers, and the white sand dunes stretch out for miles like crystal waves.

"Maybe in time," she says, "you can come visit."

Never.

"Maybe," I say.

She's crying when she calls back later. "You should see all the stars here," she says.

"It was Jim who liked stars," I remind her.

They find her dead of a massive heart attack in a bed in the Desert Rose Motel, Cheetos blowing around in the whirlpool of air from the air conditioner. They find a letter she has been writing to me. It is ten pages long.

"I want you to know how sorry I am, Medina. I didn't think everything would turn out like this," it starts out. I stop reading. I take the letter and fold it into threes. I put it in a drawer, under my brother's letters. Then I take it out again and fold it deep inside the warmth of a winter sweater.

I tell myself I'll read it when it gets cold, sometime.

⌒⌒⌒

The money from the sale of the house is mine, my father says.

"I want you to have it for the future."

He and Ava are long broken up now. His new girlfriend is a Chinese radiologist. The last one was a blond accountant.

"I'm only going to date women with jobs," he assures me. "No more Ava Adares."

I say nothing to him about Ava or Adrian Adare. I only tell him the details of my life that don't matter.

He tells me all about my mother as she was, filling in gaps with stories.

"She was lovely when I met her. God, she was beautiful then."

He talks about her as if she were a vase, a chandelier.

But when he talks about my brother we hold each other tight.

∽∽∽

I surf the waves of Santa Barbara, wearing my brother's lucky hat.

My father has become more superstitious, worrying a lot, calling twice a day, driving up to visit every weekend. He sends me thick medical studies on nutrition and pamphlets on fire safety and self-defense. He brings me a St. Christopher medal and some Indian malachite for good luck against sharks and earthquakes. To make him happy, I wear the hat and the medal, I knock three times on wood and promise him I'll be safe. Then I escape and go surfing.

He comes down to the shore, watching me paddle and take off. When I wave to him, he swims out to meet me, wearing a shiny new pair of silver trunks. He hovers around while I wait for a wave.

"You don't have a wet suit, Dad, you'll get sick," I tell him.

"Maybe I could learn to surf," he says. "We could do it together like you and Jim did."

Then he asks me if he can try my board and paddles furiously toward the next wave lineup, flailing his arms, fighting the current.

I touch his arm, treading water, and say, "Dad, if you're going to surf, you have to go slow. Remember, you can't win against the ocean."

Later, we talk. He asks me how I've changed so much in a year, how I've gotten so calm. We're lying on a big black towel under the night sky, looking at the endless spray of warm stars. My father is worried that I'm alone too much; he thinks I should come back, move in with him. I tell him I can't, I like to surf here at night, alone. As we look up at the new, bright star near Andromeda, I smile, pointing.

"See, I pretend that one is Jim."

Then I explain why I'm never lonely when I'm in the ocean—I talk to my brother while I surf. I tell my father Jim can see me every night in his wet suit, looking good on a wave.

Then I point out my mother, a new little star behind Jupiter, but close enough to watch what's going on. I tell my father I talk to her sometimes, too.

"I fought for her, Daddy, all the tribes of Palos Verdes. None of it matters anymore."

"So you're really okay?" he asks, hopefully.

"Sure," I say, not looking at him.

Later I swim far out from the shore. I wave to my father before diving under the black water. Then I scream as loud as I can.

❧❧❧

Adrian has grown up. He tells me he has a beard now, he describes it as mammal-like. He tells me there is no one else, no other girls. He tells me his mother took my father's cash parting gift and had extensive plastic surgery. He tells me she looks like a Palos Verdes type now. Her new husband is a gynecologist; he is short, a little shy. A little guy.

"They say they are happy," he writes, *"whatever that means."*

I write back: *"If you want to come, I'll be in Palos Verdes for two days. We can surf the bay one last time. Come on Saturday the seventh, to the house. We're having an auction."*

❧❧❧

There are fancy people gawking at our furniture, opening closets, looking at our clothes, bidding on our piano. There is wine and cheese on the table in the foyer. Palos Verdes people have turned out en masse, in a large show of support for us. I've asked my father not to come.

"Whatever," I say when the estate-sale executor asks for my approval on a price.

I hear people whispering the Mason story. Suicide, mental hospital, crazy. They stand together like sheep, smiling at me shyly from across the floor.

I hear Marge Paxton say, "It's like, an American tragedy."

Skeezer offers to buy my brother's surfboard for forty dollars.

"Never," I tell the executor. "Not in this lifetime."

The surf is good when Adrian and I go out. Four feet and clean. Still I struggle on my brother's two-fin board.

The boys don't throw rocks at Adrian, or heckle him, or slash his tires. They make a clean, respectful swathe for us when we paddle out, letting us line up first.

"The difference is," I tell Adrian, "I have money now."

Some things are no different. We surf for two hours, until the light is gone and the first stars appear.

"See that star?" I say. "Jim gave it to me."

He looks at the star, the brightest, bluish one, and nods.

The house is empty, dark, huge, after all the people leave. Adrian and I spend the night in the pool area, lying under the stars. He falls asleep on a deck chair. I stay awake, looking for constellations, lying on my brother's board as it eddies in the chlorine current. Night birds fly past in gentle curved formations. I watch them, tracing their graceful flexions with my finger.

My whole life I've wanted to be graceful. Sometimes when I was alone in the pool, I used to do a freestyle water ballet, kicking my legs and swirling my hair around, feeling beautiful, pretending millions of people were watching.

Jim used to say that water makes everybody beautiful.

At sunrise I do a wave check, but instead of going down to the shore, I watch from on top of the trail as the Bayboys file into the water, joking and laughing, throwing seaweed at each other. They laugh and laugh, telling the same old jokes, comfortable with each other; a tribe.

Watching the surfers, loneliness comes over me like a wave.

"Hello surfer girl," Adrian says quietly, awake now, handing me a towel.

He waits at the deck with fresh, warm breakfast croissants, wearing his nice reading glasses. We sit on the concrete ledge, and he shows me the book he's been studying, *Animals of North America.* He tells me it's a book I'd like, then turns to the chapter about desert tortoises and begins reading it out loud. All of a sudden I feel sick. I tell him I don't want to hear anything about animals, especially how tortoises get to live for one hundred fifty years. He looks at me, puzzled, for a long time.

～⌒～⌒～

The couple who buy the house at Via Neve are young: he's a corporate lawyer, she wears plaid Eddie Bauer slacks. They have a young, brown-haired son with huge blue eyes.

When I return to Palos Verdes in December, I knock on the familiar arched door, ask the couple if I can use the old trail to get down to the bay. They argue for a moment in hushed tones while I stand on the doorstep. The woman is afraid that I'll ruin the newly planted ice plant, but the man says, "Jesus, Amy, don't be so goddamned heartless." Then he smiles apologetically, lets me walk through the backyard in the muted winter sun. The woman squints at my surfboard, watching carefully, making sure I don't destroy the landscape. The little boy waves to me from the big bay window.

I pretend I don't see him.

Just before sunset, the big winter waves reach their peak. I take my brother's board, swim for a wave, ride it to the shore, and paddle out again. I kiss its nose once and then push it away as hard as I can, watching until an undertow smashes it against the breakwall. It flips high in the air and lands on its belly, shattering into mounds of resin and pale polyurethane foam.

I tread water for a while, waiting until Jim's star comes out, so I can say one last good-bye from the bay. I'll be surfing in Hawaii soon. After that, Bali, Java, Thailand. I have no itinerary, no plans to return.

I'm going to surf until I die.

As the sun sets, the brown-haired boy is still watching from the window. I wave at him slowly from the water, then give him the hang-loose sign. The boy waves back, excited. He keeps waving, even as I swim back to the shore. I give him the thumbs-up sign.

No one knows I'm crying.